JUSTICE
PREVAILS

An IMPS Romance Book 1

by

Bambi Sommers

CHAPTER ONE

OVER THE RIVER and through the woods...she couldn't help but think of that old song every time she came this way. Murphy Wells' aunt had always lived on the edge of this beautiful forest and her home had always been one of her favorite childhood memories. And the drive on this road always brought to mind that song. As she drove, she remembered being a young girl, spending hours in the lush back yard jutting up to the edge of the forest. Murphy reminisced about the abundance of birds, squirrels and rabbits and how she would always pretend they were friends coming to see only her. Of course, it always helped that she would sneak carrots and whatever goodies she could find from her aunt's kitchen to share with them! One of her most cherished memories was when she turned sixteen and would practice her driving skills on this very road. It was cut through the forest and they had worked around what trees they could. This made it mostly covered in a beautiful leafy canopy. This time of year was especially beautiful with all of its fall colors overhead. Hence, the song in her head.

Losing herself in her musings, it came as a shock when she rounded a corner and saw a man squatting down by the side of the road looking closely at the big motorcycle in front of him. Being that this road was used almost exclusively by the people who lived back toward the forest, this site struck her as strange. Was he lost? Did his motorcycle break down? Did he need help? She pulled up behind him, hit her flashers, and got out of the car. Luckily, she thought to herself, she had worn flat ankle boots so walking on the gravel at the side of the road was no problem. She would have been mortified if she fell on her ass in front of this guy!

The first thing she noticed was the color of the bike. It was silver in a way that made it look like it was entirely made of chrome. She imagined seeing it flying past on the road. It would look somewhat ethereal.

As she approached, she found it odd that he never raised his head to acknowledge her. He had to know she was there. He couldn't have missed the sound of her tires crunching on gravel. "Hi" she said. Nothing. *Really?* She cleared her throat rather loudly. "Hello" she tried again. The man grunted! Seriously! He grunted! Hmmmm. "Did you break down?" The least he could do was look up at her. Silence. "Anything I can do to help? Call someone, maybe?" She wasn't giving up yet. He let out one of the most frustrated sighs Murphy had ever head as he slowly – very slowly – stood. Yikes! This guy had to be about six three with shoulders so wide he could block the sun. And that's when he turned to look at her. Oh. My. God. Be careful what you wish for. Those eyes locked on Murphy and she could not move.

They reminded her of a wolf's eyes. Silver. *Silver!* She'd never seen anything like them and couldn't seem to look away! He held her gaze for what...a few seconds? A minute? It could have been days for all she knew. Time just seemed to stand still. When he finally spoke, his voice was so low, it came out more of a rumble against her chest. "No." No? What? What was the question? Oh yeah, she had offered to call someone for him. He broke his stare and oh so slowly lowered himself back down on his haunches and turned back towards that ghostly bike.

What the hell? All she was trying to do was help and he was dismissing her? Oh, hell no! No matter how breathtakingly handsome he was, just no! "Well then", Murphy's eyes lasered into him, "seeing how you don't need any help, I'll just be on my way. It's just that we don't get too many Neanderthals in these parts, and I just wanted to see one for myself! You know, up close and personal!" She turned on her heel and with a flip of long blond hair, walked, no, stormed, back to her car. She thought she heard a small rumble coming from him before she slammed the car door but she couldn't be sure. She gave him one of her best glares before pulling out onto the road, but the handsome bastard never even looked in her direction.

Get the fuck away from here. Justice growled the unsaid words as she walked away. *Now, Joseph, come show your ugly mug so I can end this once and for all...*

CHAPTER TWO

IT'S BEEN THREE MONTHS since she's seen 'silver eyes' but she thought of him often. What red blooded girl wouldn't? It started at those beat up, dusty biker boots under worn, soft-looking jeans, then up that broad chest to his shoulders. And what shoulders! It just wasn't fair to her libido for him to look that good and be such a giant douche! Ah, but those eyes! They appeared like lasers under those dark brows and then there was a mass of dark hair which curled around the collar of his black leather jacket. And when he finally did turn towards her, she saw what looked like a day's worth of beard shadow across that strong jaw. Geez! Really? At the time, she thought she only noticed his eyes, but reflecting back, realized she had somehow taken in almost the whole package...almost. Had he not been such a ginormous asshat, she could have had quite a vivid fantasy life going on with this one. Oh, who was she kidding? She didn't care how much of an ass he'd been, the fantasy just kept coming! All it took was for her to imagine those eyes on her and, yep, there it was!

It was easy to live a fantasy life when you didn't really have a romantic one. Sure, she'd had the occasional fling but nothing ever felt lasting. She had her fair share of male friends and colleagues but no one did it for her. And, evidently, she didn't do it for anyone else, either. But she felt pretty good about her life in general. Working for herself in her small coffee shop was exactly where she wanted to be. Plus, she had a wonderful circle of friends and customers to keep her company. So, at the end of the day, she was more than ok.

It was Saturday and she was at her coffee shop, her place of business. She loved it there. She bought the building with some inheritance money when her mother died four years ago. While her mom was still alive, there was a low point in her life, trying to build a career out of something she had gone to college for but later found out she hated. She and her mother, Joy, had a long heart to heart conversation about what she should do when her mother suggested she change careers and go with something she loved. Two days after their talk, her mother died suddenly of a massive heart attack. No warning at all. Just emptiness. Her father had been gone now for over twenty years, having died from a surgery complication, so being the only living family, she received a nice inheritance and took her mother's words to heart. She loved coffee, loved making people happy, and most of all, loved her mother. Hence the opening of The Joyful Cafe.

The sun was shining brightly this October morning making the butter-yellow walls extra welcoming and cheerful. The light filled the space coming through the row of windows lining the front of the shop. She'd had muntin bars installed in the windows so they looked like individual panels with beautiful white strips of wood separating each one. She kept them bare, with the exception of a pair of beautiful pale green curtains framing the ends of the window row. They laid in straight panels with the bottoms just touching the gleaming hardwood floor. The café tables and chairs were bar height and left bare of tablecloths so their highly polished wood could shine through. Everything was kept simple by design. She had, however, allowed herself one big indulgence when deciding on the decorating. She had hired an artist friend of hers (her best friend, Cassie, as a matter of fact) to paint big, beautiful murals on the three walls without windows. These murals were of huge brightly colored cups filled with various types of steaming coffees. There was expresso with rich, dark color, mocha lattes with intricate designs in the foam floating on top, along with mugs with whipped cream dripping down their sides onto matching saucers. It was a site to behold and made The Joyful Café's décor impressive and unique.

It was 9am and the café was bustling. There were only two out of the ten tables available. Weekdays, most customers took their coffee to go, but being that it was Saturday, people had more time to sit and relax. Some were alone and reading the paper, some were typing furiously on their laptops and some were with friends laughing in carefree conversation.

As Murphy made her way through the tables checking on everyone's cups for refills, she felt a hand touch her elbow. She turned to see Mr. O'Brien. "Well, good morning, Mr. O'Brien. Anything I can get for you?" Mr. O'Brien must have been ninety if he was a day. His face had so many lines, it looked like a roadmap but his pale blue eyes still had a mischievous twinkle and his smile was highly contagious. "Nope", he replied. "Just thought since you were standing here, I'd let you know that cohort of yours is just about to walk in the door!"

With that, the little bell above the door jingled and, yep, in came Cassie Thompson like the mini tornado she was! Cassie had been Murphy's best friend since college and was an artist extraordinaire! Not only had she made The Joyful Cafe's décor one of a kind, she had painted murals for the town square, other businesses and had sold a too numerous to mention amount of paintings that were hanging in homes and businesses across neighboring cities. She always arrived breathless with her mass of beautiful red curls bobbing around her shoulders and that bright smile always in place. Standing at only five feet two inches, she was small of statute but she was a force to be reckoned with. Men of all ages turned to watch her walk in and she made sure she had a smile for each of them! Cassie was one of those women who other women couldn't help but like and men couldn't help but lust after.

"Murph!" she called out in that sultry voice of hers, "you'll never believe what just happened to me! You'll never believe it!"

Before Murphy even had a chance to reply, Cassie grabbed her friend's forearm and started to drag her towards the booth she kept in the back of the café for special reservations, but mostly for her and her friends. Before dragging her too far though, Cassie stopped abruptly, turned on her heel, and gave a little wink and hello to Mr. O'Brien, who I swear blushed a little. Incredible!

"Murph, remember that appointment I had today with a Riley Harrison?" Before Murphy could even reply (sensing a theme here?), Cassie rambled on. "You remember, he called me after seeing the painting I did for Mrs. Neal, and asked if I would meet with him to discuss doing a painting for his house? Anyway, I show up at the address he gave me and guess where it was!" Thinking she was going to take a breath here and allow a guess, Murphy took in a breath and started to say "I can't…"

"Oh, you'll never guess in a million years!" *So much for my turn*, Murphy thought. "It was the penthouse apartment in the Carlton Arms! Holy Shit! I've never even had reason to walk in the lobby of that place, let alone been in the penthouse! And…" she continued as she tucked a curl behind her ear, "you'll never guess what he does for a living! He manages that band…oh, you know…what's their name?...ummm" she started waving her arms around and snapping her fingers like that would make her remember. "Oh, it'll come to me. Anyhoo, he commissioned me to do a piece for his penthouse for a buttload of money!" Was she going to finally pause? Annnnd, that would be a no. "So, what do ya think? You haven't said a word!"

Murphy's mouth twitched at the corner trying to keep a laugh from escaping. "Really? I guess I just didn't have anything to say!"

Cassie stared at her incredulously for a minute then scrunched up her face and said "Oh. Sarcasm. I get it. Droll. Very droll, indeed."

Murphy laughed out loud. "I know you don't even realize when you're doing it, but you sure can go on! What I think is...I don't know why you're so surprised when you get these commissions. Your reputation obviously precedes...."

Murphy was cut off by the ringing of Cassie's cell phone. Cassie looked at the phone but didn't recognize the number. She always answered anyway. After all, it might be a new client.

"Hello? Oh, well hello Mr. Harrison." (hmmm, did Cassie's voice just get a little huskier?) "Oh well then, Riley, yes, um, call me Cassie. Tonight?" (She darted a quick look at Murphy, whose eyebrows had raised so high they were practically at her hairline). "Well, my friend, Murphy, and I were going to have a drink at The Raven's Claw." At this surprising news, Murphy started shaking her head in a silent no, no, no motion but Cassie raised a hand in a gesture that said 'don't even think about it' and carried on. "You're welcome to join us if you'd like. Really? Yes, um, I think that would be terrific! Ok then, see you there. Goodbye."

"Are you crazy?" Murphy was in a bellowing mood until she noticed heads turning in her direction from her customers. Whoops! Forgot where she was for a minute. In a lower bellowing voice, she continued, "We did not have plans tonight! Well actually, *I* did! I was planning on catching up on some much-needed sleep! You know, Cass, as in going home, getting into my jammies, pouring a wonderfully relaxing glass of wine...just thinking about it makes me happy! I am certainly not going out with you and Richey Rich!"

"Hey now. There's no cause for insulting the poor guy. We don't know if he's as wealthy as Richey Rich. Just hoping. Come on Murphy, you have to go. I don't really know this guy but it could be really fun! When was the last time you put on some lipstick and got your ass out of your house? And before you even say it, going to the grocery store doesn't count!"

Murphy grumbled something that Cassie didn't quite hear and that was probably a good thing. "No. Just no. I'm not going! I have a new book I've been dying to start! Besides, what fun would I have, being a third wheel in your little party?"

Cassie's cheeks pinkened with this statement. "Well, actually, um…you wouldn't b…."

"Ooooooh no!" Murphy was gaining momentum now that she was beginning to realize just what Cassie was saying – or trying not to say. "He's bringing a friend for me, isn't he?"

"Well, not exactly for yo…."

"Just stop right there, Cassie Thompson! I've known you too long to believe that that was nothing but a craptastic lie! And you're happy about it! Just in case you and Richey hit it off, you won't feel so bad ditching me because his friend will be there! No! Absolutely not!"

Cassie's shoulders fell a little at this last statement. She really wanted to get to know Riley and this was so perfect! She could get to know him a bit and Murphy would get out and have some fun for a change. She wasn't expecting anything meaningful to come of any of this. It was just drinks for fuck's sake! She picked up her phone to text a cancel. She certainly wasn't going alone now that she already told Riley she had plans.

Murphy hadn't missed the slight resignation in Cassie and she felt bad she had jumped at her friend. What would it hurt to have an hour or two with a guy she would never have to see again if it made Cassie happy? "Ok. Don't cancel. I'll go. But just this once and don't expect me to stay out dancing all night! That book is definitely calling my name and so is some good sleep!"

Cassie's arms came up and wrapped around her friend's neck. "Thank you, Murph. You won't be disappointed. If his friend is half of what Riley is, you definitely won't be."

"That good, huh? And, what's so special about this Riley, besides having too much money?"

Cassie had that pink in her cheeks again but this time, it had a little more heat in it. "Hmmmm.. short, blond hair, the bluest eyes I've ever seen, like the ocean, ya know, with that touch of aqua? He's tall. I'd say maybe six two and athletically built...long and lean." She finished this last part with a faraway look in her eyes and a more pronounced breathiness in her voice. "And you know there is no such thing as *too* much money!"

Murphy gave and exaggerated eye roll and laughed. "Ok, well, get outta here and let me finish out my day."

Cassie promised to pick Murphy up at 8 o'clock sharp, gave her a quick peck on the cheek, winked again at Mr. O'Brien and left the café the same way she entered, in a swirl of pure Cassie, smiling and happy.

CHAPTER THREE

THE RAVEN'S CLAW was bustling, even though it was still early. Cassie and Murphy had purposely arrived before the guys so they could see them walk in the door. Cassie looked beautiful in grayed jeans that fit her curves like a second skin. These jeans were tucked into three-inch red over-the-knee boots that made little tick-tick noises over the hardwood floors when she walked. She had thrown on a black sweater with a low neckline that showcased her cleavage and said sexy not slutty, in a way that only Cassie could pull off. She topped all this with red earrings that dangled close to her shoulders and several red bangles that jangled on her wrist.

Murphy was dressed in her favorite pair of black skinny jeans tucked into flat dark green ankle boots with silver buckles. This was topped with a long dark green tunic that flowed when she moved. Her 'girls' weren't quite as prominently displayed as Cassie's but then again, she wasn't the one looking to get laid. Right?

They grabbed a booth across the room so they could keep an eye on the door. The waitress had been around and brought drinks and they had settled into some comfortable conversation. The band was milling around the stage checking on their various instruments, making sure everything was in good shape before they were to go on at nine.

"They're here!" Cassie reached out to touch her friend's arm but was a little too enthusiastic as she bumped Murphy's purse and sent it spiraling to the floor. Murphy leaned out of the booth to pick up said bag when she saw four legs walk up. Two of those legs obviously belonged to Cassie's date. They had on what had to be tailor made trousers over a pair of Brooks Brothers loafers shined so bright you could see your reflection. And what was that? Alligator? Wow! That's when she saw a very large masculine hand reach down and pick up a lipstick which had taken a tumble out of her bag. She took a quick peek at *his* shoes. No, it couldn't be. No. No. No! It was a pair of well-worn black biker boots surrounded by...you guessed it, jeans! This couldn't be happening. Well, she couldn't stay down here forever (could she?) so she slowly pulled herself back up into the seat noticing him all the way up. Please don't have silver eyes! Please don't have silver eyes! She scanned very tall legs to see slim hips and... don't look at his package...oops! Looked! Nice! Trim waist and, yep, going up into broad shoulders with dark hair just brushing his collar. And silver eyes! Damn it!

He held the lipstick out to her not saying a word. Just lifted one eyebrow as though asking if she wanted it or not.

She hadn't noticed until this moment that Cassie was receiving a kiss on the cheek from her handsome friend and turning to do introductions.

"Murphy, this is Riley Harrison. Riley, meet my best friend in the whole world, Murphy Wells." Riley took her outstretched hand and brought it to his lips to kiss the back of it. Very nice. That didn't happen often. Then he turned to do his introductions.

"Cassie, this is Justice Coulter. Justice, this is Cassie Thompson. She's going to be doing a fine art piece for my living room and possibly more...uh...rooms." Was that a twinkle in his eye as the innuendo hit Cassie. "And this beautiful lady is...."

He was cut off by Justice's deep baritone. "No introduction's necessary. Ms. Wells already knows me. In fact, she has her own little nickname for me, don't you, hon? Neanderthal."

Murphy felt the flush of color start at her neckline and slowly rise up her face. Wait! Why should she feel guilty? All she did was stop that day on the road and try to help him. *He* was the one who should be apologizing! Justice seemed to be enjoying her discomfort, if the gleam in his eye meant anything. Well, she refused to be uncomfortable around this arrogant, no-good, trouble making....

Murphy's thoughts were interrupted when a strangled little sound came from Cassie. She looked over to find Cassie's mouth hanging open as she looked from Justice to Murphy. Cassie had never quite seen that color on Murphy's cheeks before. She glanced at Riley, expecting his mouth to be hanging open, too, but instead saw an expression on his face she didn't quite recognize. Was that humor that had his mouth twisted in a little bow? Did he know what the hell was going on here? And, would someone mind telling her?

Justice's eyes never left Murphy's even though he knew his buddy was holding in a laugh. He had told Riley about his previous encounter with the woman along the side of the road but, of course, he had no idea what her name was or that he would ever see her again, especially in circumstances such as these. He knew someone should break the awkward silence but damned if it would be him. Hmmm, maybe he was an asshole!

Murphy cleared her throat and her eyes rose to meet his. "Well, Mr. Neander...aww...I mean, Mr. Coulter, it's so lovely to see you again. I was afraid that maybe our last encounter was one and done." No one in the immediate vicinity could miss the sarcasm dripping from her words.

It was Riley's turn to step in. "Miss Wells, may I call you Murphy?" Murphy's head nodded slightly. "Well then, Murphy, I apologize on behalf of my friend. He does appear to be dragging his knuckles a bit now, doesn't he?" Justice turned those silver eyes on his friend as a corner of his mouth tilted upward. Riley looked back at Justice for a split second then motioned for the ladies to move over in the seats to clear some room for them to sit. Cassie moved over immediately and glared at Murphy when she hesitated, seemingly trying to make up her mind as to whether she was going to move over or run. She gave a little shake of her head and moved over.

"Would someone like to clue me in on what's happening here?" Cassie was surprised she had to ask. It wasn't like Murphy not to share. They usually talked about everything. Murphy looked at Justice and nodded her head towards Cassie. She actually wanted *him* to do the honors?

Riley caught the head nod and looked across the table at Justice. "Looks like you're up, big man."

Now with all eyes on Justice, he couldn't see his way out of this one. He brought that big paw up and pinched the bridge of his nose as though this was the most difficult thing he ever had to do. Then he opened those gorgeous eyes of his and with a heavy sigh of frustration, started talking. "I was mindin' my own business and tweaking my bike's engine along the side of the road when Miss do-gooder here stopped to see if I needed help." He gestured in her direction with his thumb as Murphy tried to interrupt but Justice carried on, speaking over her. "Ya see, I was concentrating and wasn't broken down. It's just easier to do certain alterations when you've had 'er runnin' for a while. Anyway, I guess I wasn't as nice as Ms. Wells thought I should be so she labeled me a Neanderthal and left in a huff. End of story."

Murphy had never heard him talk enough to realize his gravelly voice had a slight southern touch to it. She had only remembered how his one word 'no' had reverberated against her chest and, if she was honest with herself, traveled south. Sitting in the booth next to him when he was saying more than one word had her girly parts sitting up and saying hello! Down, girls!

"Ok. First of all, I am not a do-gooder, I just travel that road frequently and usually don't see strangers, especially ones pulled off the side of the road so I thought you might need help. Ok, that does kind of make me sound like a do-gooder but really, I wouldn't do that if I hadn't known the area as well as I do. And just because you didn't need my help doesn't give you the right to be an asshat!"

Justice broke out in laughter and Oh. My. God. What a site that was! He had beautiful, straight white teeth that shone from under that scruff on his handsome face and the sound of his laughter boomed through her until...well, panties dropped! What the hell was the matter with her? She didn't even like this guy!

Murphy's ear picked up Riley's laughter then. She had forgotten there was anyone there besides her and Justice.

Riley was almost doubled over in the booth, holding his sides, laughing. "Did you really just call him an asshat? Man, Justice, this woman has got your number!"

As the laughter started to die down in the booth, Cassie finally found her voice. "Well, I'm not sure exactly what happened but what I do know is that it's unusual for Murphy to act like she's acting right now." Cassie gave Murphy a what the fuck look and didn't miss her eye roll that was given to her in return. "How about we just all start again. Let's order drinks and try to behave ourselves." She drew her eyebrows down about as far as they would go to have a look at Murphy, then Justice. Then she turned her eyes to Riley and smiled that dazzling smile of hers. Riley smiled back at Cassie's sweet face and was instantly glad he had called her. There was just something about her that appealed to him. She was all soft curves and woman. He started up a conversation about the painting she was going to do for him. He figured that would be a safe subject after all the mess so far and he really did want to get to know her better.

While Riley and Cassie lost themselves in conversation, Murphy figured it was about time she and Neanderthal man put aside their differences. If Riley and Cassie hit it off as well as she suspected they would, then she and Justice would probably be seeing more of each other than they wanted so she may as well make peace with it. "So, listen. I'm sorry I called you a Neanderthal. That wasn't really a fair assessment since I really don't know you and it just wasn't nice of me. You just made me mad when you wouldn't even acknowledge me that day on the road. And since it looks like we may have to see each other again being that..." she gave a little nod of her head at the two across the booth with their heads together like there was no one else in the world but them, "our friends seem to be hitting it off, let's call a truce, and start over. What do you say?"

The hopeful look in her eyes hit Justice's heart in a way he hadn't felt in a while. The stupid organ did a little flip backward and then flipped forward again. Holy Hell! What was that? He kept his face in check, not wanting her to see the shock there, and turned those silver eyes on her. "Well, I guess I owe you an apology, too. I was caught up in what I was doing with my bike and to be honest, it was hard for me not to think of you as a nuisance at that moment. So, I'm sorry if I hurt your feelings or scared you. I suppose I should work on being nicer."

Wow! That was some apology. She didn't think he had it in him but she wouldn't bother saying that out loud or they would never make any headway. "I never said I was *scared*. What I said was I was mad. But that's beside the point. We're gonna let that go. So, what do you do for a living?"

She noticed his eyes dart around the room and his lips form a thin line. And had she really noticed his lips before? The bottom was lusciously full while the top one was a little thinner and, wow, could she get lost in the thought of how they would feel on her, nibbling...ahhhh. What? Was he talking? No, he was looking at her like he expected a response. Yikes! What was the question? "Um, I'm sorry. What did you say?" Now those lips curved into the sexiest little smirk she'd ever seen. Wait! That's how she got distracted the first time!

He continued to smirk at her for a moment as though he could read her mind and she noticed his eyes skimming down to check out her own lips. Then it seemed as though he caught himself and looked around the room before lighting back on her eyes. "So, what do you do for fun, Wells?"

"Fun? I guess I work. That's fun for me. And I read. And I...wow, I never realized how boring I sound."

"Boring?" He let his eyes travel down the length of her sitting in that booth so very close to him. "You may be a lot of things, Wells, but boring would certainly not be one of them. Why is work so much fun? What do you do?"

Now the light was back in her blue eyes and he could see the passion she possessed. "I own The Joyful Café. It's a little coffee place over on 13th Street. It's not much, but it's what makes me happy. I've built up a loyal little following there and I like seeing the familiar faces every day. What about you? You never said what it is that you do for a living." At least she hoped he hadn't.

His eyes did that darting thing again. What was that? Did I hit a nerve or something? "Didn't I? Well, I get by."

This man certainly knew how to clam up when he wanted to. Something was up but she wouldn't press if he didn't want to say. I just hoped whatever he did for a living was at least legal. "Ok then, what do *you* do for fun?"

Fun must be easier to talk about then work because he opened up at this question. "I tinker with my bike on back roads, as you know." This was said with a wry smile and a low chuckle that made her insides do that little butterfly thing. "And, you know, I like long walks on the beach, romance novels, picking wildflowers..." his smile was huge now and it slowly sank in that he was messing with her.

"What the hell are you talking about? You're about as close to the kind of man who likes those things as I am to the kind of girl who could fix your motorcycle! So, what are you going on about?"

His laugh was deep and rumbling. Damn! Why did she feel that reverberate in her chest so much? She'd heard deep voices before but none affected her like this! "Just thought I'd see how closely you were listening, Wells."

"Oh, I was listening all right. You just weren't saying anything worth listening to." Here we go again.

He swung those eyes on her again and she wished he stop doing that. She needed some warning for those eyes. "I'll try to be more entertaining from now on." Ok. Sarcasm. She definitely got sarcasm. "What I'd really like to do is take my bike out for a ride around the lake tomorrow. Make sure I tweaked her in all the right places. You up for that, Wells?"

What? Was she hearing him right? Was he asking her out? *Yes, please!* "I've never been on a motorcycle before."

"Never?" His look was incredulous. "Don't worry. I'll be gentle." More sarcasm? She frowned until his big hand came over to touch the top of her own and bam! She swore she saw a spark! She didn't get to see if it had really happened because he withdrew his hand as fast as he could. When she raised her eyes to his, she saw that his eyes were on the spot where he had just touched her. So, he felt it too?

"All right, then. I'm game. Should be fun." She wasn't sure who she was trying to convince, him or herself? But the café was closed on Sunday and a ride with a gorgeous man may be just what she needed.

The rest of the evening was spent with drinks and small talk among the four of them. When it came to calling it a night, Riley bent to give Murphy a little peck on the cheek and she noticed that he kissed Cassie full on the mouth. Yep! They most certainly were hitting it off! Good. She wanted Cassie to be happy and Riley did seem like a really nice guy, even though, the jury was still out on his choice of friends. Hmmmm. Didn't say much for her though. She was the one going riding with this friend tomorrow.

CHAPTER FOUR

"WHAT'S THAT LOOK on your face?" Justice was trying to get comfortable in the passenger seat of Riley's Lamborghini Huracan. Yeah, he got why Riley loved this car. It was sleek. It was beautiful. And it was fast! All the things he loved about his motorcycle. However, the one thing he did not love about this car was getting in and trying to fit. Justice was a big man, bigger than most, and sports cars were not usually built for his size. This one felt like a sardine can.

Riley was busy shifting gears and trying to keep the shit eating grin off his face. "You are a true fucking piece of work." Now that grin was a full-fledged in-your-face smirk with a side of cocky. "So, you meet this gorgeous woman on the side of the road who, by the way, is also nice, and you had to know that when she actually stopped because she thought you were in trouble, and you were a total...now let's see, what did she call it? Oh yes. Asshat!" Riley was laughing. Laughing his ass off!

"Yea, but..."

"Oh no. I'm not even *close* to being done!" Riley didn't even let Justice get a few words in. "And you did this because, if I know you at all, you figured you'd never see her again and besides, you don't have time for anything but a quick screw to scratch an itch! And if you think it's a possibility the girl has a brain, forget it! She's not worth your time. Because, if she has a brain, she'll expect more than what you're willing – or able, according to you – to give. Am I right or am I right?"

This time, Riley paused and Justice saw his opening. "Yea, but…"

"Not yet. Not done. You realize that I like Cassie and I haven't liked anyone for what seems like a hell of a long time! Then you come along and almost fuck it up for me! It's one thing to fuck up your life. Yes, get that scowl off your face, buddy. It doesn't work on me. I know you too well. But to almost fuck mine up, too? Oh, Hell no! You just have to admit that you got lucky! Murphy seems like a reasonable woman and I hope the hell you apologized for being such a jerk!"

Another pause. "Can I talk now?" Justice's face was stone when Riley finally nodded. "I, in fact, did apologize and she and I are going riding tomorrow."

It was a good thing Riley treasured his car so much because if he was driving anything else he may have wrecked.

Shock showed in his eyes at the news he had just heard. "You saying that gorgeous creature agreed to an actual date with a cretin like yourself?" Oh yeah. Riley was having fun with this one.

"Yeah, smart ass. It's Beauty and the Beast all over again. Looks like I didn't fuck it up after all. For you *or* me. And yes, before you go all girly on me and start wanting to paint each other's nails, she's never been on a bike before so I thought I'd take her on a long ride around the lake."

Riley was silent a moment. It wasn't like Justice to actually want to spend time with a woman unless it was sex time. Hmmm. And he didn't remember Justice ever taking a woman on his bike. He needed a moment to think this one over. It didn't slip by Justice that his friend was silent. Justice, himself, knew this wasn't his normal MO when it came to women, and he wasn't quite sure what to think of it himself. He only knew that *this* woman, this one particular woman, was already under his skin. The thought of her now so close to him in that booth, smelling like some exotic spice, had him trying to adjust himself, and that was a feat for such a large man in such a small car! Fact was, he'd been hiding a half mast all evening! Murphy, with her long blond hair, killer blue eyes, and a long lean body... well now. What the hell was he going to do?

"Having a little trouble there, my friend?" Riley had noticed Justice's discomfort and couldn't help making fun.

"Shut the fuck up!"

Murphy didn't sleep well that night. She and Cassie hadn't talked much on the way home. They had both admitted to having a great time and Murphy knew Cassie was lost in thoughts of Riley. They would talk about it another time. This suited Murphy fine as she, herself, was lost in some thoughts, too. She had agreed to go on a motorcycle ride with a man she barely knew and the craziest part of this plan was that she just didn't care! Maybe it was time to put herself out there a bit. She wasn't sure if this was the right man to put herself out there with but then again, did anyone ever really know for sure? There was one thing that remained in the back of her mind. She never got an answer to what he did for living. Did she? She got distracted by those lips and wasn't sure he had told her! Then when she got her courage up to ask again, he said he got by. Damn it! Now, how the hell was she supposed to ask him again when he might have already told her and she missed it because she was thinking about those lips nibbling on her neck, then her shoulders, down to her breasts then...Oh. My. God. Stop! Maybe she should have just taken him to bed tonight and got it over with! But then again, maybe she wanted a little bit more.

CHAPTER FIVE

THE NEXT MORNING came with sunshine and temperatures in the high 60's. Perfect biking weather, she guessed. Justice was supposed to pick her up at eleven and told her they would stop for lunch during the ride. He said he knew the perfect place. She awoke early and was able to get some of her normal Sunday work done. This was always the day she tried to catch up on laundry, house cleaning and reading. The reading would have to wait but she finished the housework and the laundry was in the dryer. She showered and dressed. Not sure what to wear, she pulled on jeans and a purple sweater and topped that off with simple silver hoop earrings and black riding boots that came to just below her knees. Not sure how cold it would be on an open bike, she laid out her favorite jean jacket and a cute little purple scarf. She was tying her hair back at the nape of her neck when she first heard it. It sounded like thunder rolling through the side streets till it pulled up directly in front of her house and stopped. The silence was a bit deafening when Justice turned the big machine off and swung his leg over it. Not being able to help herself, she was watching from behind her living room curtains. He was nimble for such a big man and had a natural swagger that was full of confidence and complete alpha male. And boy, did that do it for her! She watched him swagger up the porch steps until he was at her front door. She was so lost in him, she actually jumped a bit when he raised that big hand to knock.

When Murphy opened the door, Justice's eyes took her in. Slowly. She was watching him intently, expecting, hoping, he would smile, but he didn't. Instead, he frowned. "Good thing I brought this." He said as he handed over a black leather jacket. "As good as you look, Wells, you'll freeze in that little thing you have on." Murphy looked at the jacket. Hmmm. Just her size. What the hell? He probably had a whole closet full of these in different sizes for all the woman he took on *rides*. She knew she was being ridiculous. He didn't belong to her! He could do whatever he wanted! He could have as many women's coats as he wanted! "Now before you get yourself all worked up about where I got that, it happens to belong to my sister. I figured she was about your size, so I stopped by her house on the way here and borrowed it for you. I didn't think you would have anything appropriate to wear since you've never ridden before." Well, that was just the sweetest thing she'd ever heard and she melted just a little...ok, a lot!

Justice helped her out of her jean jacket and on with the leather one. His eyes, once again, slowly took her in. This time he did smile and, boy oh boy, those white teeth under those lips and stubble. Did she actually sigh out loud? When his smile got a little wider, and a lot more wicked, she realized she had. *Get it together, Murph!* He escorted her out the door and, after she locked up, they walked down the sidewalk towards the curb where he parked his bike. Murphy looked at it like it was a snake coiled and ready to strike. "It won't bite, you know." She looked at Justice and noticed the smirk he wasn't even trying to hide. "Here. Also, my sister's. She and her husband ride, too." She took the helmet he handed her and promptly put it atop her head. He pushed the top of it down to make sure it was secure then put his on while she fussed with the strap. He then swung his leg over the beast and scooted forward a bit so she could get on behind him. One second passed. Two. Ten? He looked over his shoulder to see what the holdup was. Murphy was eyeing the seat not quite sure what to do. Justice's heart melted just a bit when he saw her standing there looking like a lost little girl. "Swing your leg over, Wells, and put yourself behind me on the seat." He heard her make some kind of sound but wasn't quite sure what it was. She raised her leg and, somewhat awkwardly, swung it over the big bike and plowed right into his back. Hmmmph! She was glad he had his back to her so he couldn't see her pleasure in being this up close and personal to him. She wiggled a bit and finally got situated. "You ok back there?" Murphy jumped a little when Justice's booming bass came through her helmet. She hadn't realized there was a speaker system built in so they could communicate without shouting.

"Y-Yes. I'm o-ok."

"All right then. Put your arms around my waist and hang on."

He wanted her to do what? He started the bike, revved it a couple of times, and pulled onto the street. Oh! Now she got it. She threw her arms around his waist and held on for dear life!

"Ah, Wells? As much as I'm enjoying this, you might want to loosen your grip just a little."

Was he laughing? More like trying not to! Ok. She loosened her grip and hoped he might talk to her a bit more. His deep voice in her ear was one of the sexiest things she had ever experienced. Of course, it could have something to do with all the maleness she was up against. Literally. He was a wall of rock hard muscle, heat and clean manly scent, like a mix of soap and leather. Yum!

They rode for a while and Murphy found herself relaxing and enjoying herself. The view around the lake was beautiful this time of year. The trees were all various shades of yellow, red and orange and those trees were reflected like beautiful mirages in the lake itself. Cassie should come out here to paint. Her thoughts were interrupted when that deep voice tickled her ear. "You're awful quiet back there. You doin' ok?"

"I'm better than ok. It's beautiful here and I'm quite enjoying the ride." He had no idea part of her enjoyment was being pressed up against his warm back. "I was just thinking Cassie should come out here to paint. She could capture the beautiful fall trees reflected in the lake."

Justice hummed his approval as he realized just how glad he was that Murphy was enjoying this. He never put women on the back of his bike. He was aware a lot of bikers did that just to impress but he never felt the need. But, somehow, he wanted to experience this with Murphy and it was even better than what he had hoped. Although, with her front against his back, he had to fight Mr. Chubby for space in his jeans or he was sure he'd have a permanent zipper imprint! He could swear he felt her nipples even through both of their leather jackets. Oh yeah. He was a perv!

"We're getting close to a little place by the lake where we can get some lunch. You hungry?"

"Always." She replied.

Justice chuckled that low rumbling sound as only he could. They rode for a little further then pulled into the parking lot of a small place called Katie's. He parked the bike and turned off the screaming engine. Murphy got off the bike only a little less awkwardly than she had gotten on. Justice immediately missed her pressed up against his back and shook his head as if that would clear the unfamiliar feeling.

He swung his leg over, removed his helmet and hung it on the bike. When he turned towards Murphy, she had removed hers, too, and was handing it to him. She pulled her hair out of its ponytail holder so she could smooth it back again and put the holder back in place. As she took the first step, she stumbled slightly and Justice's big arms came up to catch her. "Whoa, there. I shoulda' warned you. After riding awhile, especially at first, your legs are bound to feel a bit wobbly. Take your time. They'll come back to you." She righted herself, stretched her back a bit and started off toward the restaurant's entrance. She was surprised when she felt Justice's warm hand at the small of her back.

CHAPTER SIX

THE BELL TINKLED over the restaurant's door as they pushed it inward and stopped in the doorway. They were looking around to choose a seat when a woman in an apron cried out and came running towards them. She jumped up and squeezed Justice's neck so hard Murphy thought he may just tumble over backwards, but he remained upright while holding the woman off her feet, and grinning extra wide. Boy what that grin did to her insides! "Why Justice Coulter, you old rascal! You sure are a sight for sore eyes! Where ya' been? Haven't seen you in a while!" Murphy may have felt a bit jealous (*really?*) but this woman's smile was so bright and she was a bit older and, by the looks of it, maybe the restaurant owner. It was hard not to immediately take a liking to her. She didn't even wait for an answer from Justice as she turned her eyes to Murphy. "And who might you be? It's about time Justice got himself a woman! I've been saying that for years!" Then she leaned in towards Murphy and in a stage whisper, said "I don't know how you captured the big guy here, but I'm sure glad you did! Now, let's find you two a seat and get some food into you, honey, you are entirely too thin!" With that, she turned and took off through the restaurant knowing we would follow. She didn't seem like the type of woman who really gave you a choice. Murphy turned to look up at Justice who raised a what are you waiting for eyebrow and motioned for her to follow Katie.

When they were seated, Justice made the introductions and they ordered with a recommendation from Katie herself. Homemade chicken noodle soup with fresh homemade rolls and real butter! Sounded perfect since they were a bit chilled from their ride.

Suddenly it was just the two of them. Even with the sound of silverware clinking on china plates, it felt a little too quiet. Justice's silver eyes met hers. He had the most concentrated stare of anyone she had ever known. She smiled up at him. "I guess you know Katie, yeah?"

His deep laugh touched her in places that had her squeezing her thighs together. She wondered if he had a clue as to what he did to her. Did she do the same to him? "Yeah, Katie and I go way back. As you now know, though, it's been awhile since I've been 'round to see her. And yes, she's always nagging me to get a woman!"

"You don't bring women here?" *Please say no.*

He did that silver stare thing at her again. Damn! He should get a patent on that! He'd make millions! He seemed uneasy with her question and shifted in the booth.

Murphy continued "I'm sorry. That really isn't any of my business. I shouldn't have asked."

"No. I don't bring women here." Well, now...that was final, wasn't it? She wondered why but knew better than to ask. "Now," he continued, "it's my turn to ask a question." She raised her brows in a sign that said go ahead. "What were you doing on Forest Road that day we met?" Hmmm. She hadn't thought he would ask that. She wasn't the stranger on that road. He was. "My aunt lives there and I was going to visit her." Justice went still. Eerily still. Murphy wanted to put a mirror under his nose to make sure he was even breathing. "Justice, are you ok?"

He narrowed that stare on her again but this time, his brows came down into a deep v. "Where, exactly, does your aunt live?"

She hesitated for a moment, then continued. "Why does it matter?"

He seemed to snap out of it then and put a small smile on his face but it somehow failed. How to get himself out of this, he wondered. "Uh. It's just that I've never known anyone to be lucky enough to live there. It seems to be a nice place. Nice and secluded. Guess I was just wondering if any of the houses were empty or ever come up for sale." Yeah, that seemed like a fairly innocent thing to ask. He hoped.

"Oh. It's a wonderful place to live. I spent a lot of time when I was younger there and now that my mother is gone I try to see my aunt as often as I can. She was my mom's sister. I don't remember any houses for sale for a long time. It seems like once someone gets a place there, they hang on to it, you know? Sometimes pass it down to the next generation. That's why I was surprised when I saw you. That's a fairly secluded stretch of road and it's normal to know everyone passing." She paused and bit her bottom lip, thinking. Justice tracked her action and felt his dick twitch. "Although, come to think of it, the house next to Aunt Ivy's cottage has been empty for a while but I think one of the grandsons must have just moved in because there's been recent activity around the old place." Did Justice tense just a little? She studied him for a moment and then figured she'd imagined it. "As a matter of fact, since you seem to like the area, I was wondering if you'd maybe want to stop by? I'd like to check on Ivy. She didn't seem quite like herself this morning when I talked to her." She had no idea how much he'd like to stop by.

After finishing what was one of the most delicious lunches Murphy had ever eaten, they said their goodbyes to Katie and rode off with promises to visit her again soon.

CHAPTER SEVEN

JOSEPH TUCKER SAT BACK in the ratty old recliner, the very seat where his grandfather had made his home when he was alive. He wondered if the guy even got up to take a piss. He couldn't recall a time in recent history the man wasn't in this chair. Joe got up to get a beer from the fridge. What the hell was he going to do? He couldn't live his life hiding out here – barely turning on a light – trying not to attract attention to himself. He wanted a real life. One where he wouldn't have to slink in the shadows. Wouldn't have to duck his head. He wanted to be able to look people in the eye, maybe find a woman, have some kids. Who knows? And he fucking deserved it! He deserved it as much as that cop! Fucking cops! That fucking asshole thought he was bigger and better than everyone else! Badder, too! Well, now he was dead. *Not feeling so high and mighty anymore, are you, dickhead?* Joseph's thoughts ran around in circles in his head and he knew he'd go insane if he continued to live like this.

Just as that last thought of insanity hit him, he heard a faraway rumbling sound. The sound was growing louder, coming nearer. That was out of the ordinary for this quiet neighborhood. He ran back to the ugly recliner where he could watch, unobserved, through the curtains. He clicked off the one dim lamp he allowed himself so he could be hidden in total darkness.

The sound was a large motorcycle with two riders. It pulled into the driveway of the pretty little yellow cottage just a short distance away. He immediately grabbed a pair of binoculars he kept on the bottom of the stand now holding his beer. He studied the pair disembarking from the bike. The first was a woman. Tall. Nicely built. Boots. Jeans. Black leather jacket. Blond hair. Pretty. Hmmm. Made his dick stir. Yea, it'd been awhile and...movement caught his eye and he turned his binoculars toward the driver. A man. A very large man. Black biker boots, jeans. Black leather jacket. Helmet. Something familiar lit up Joseph's insides. What? What was he sensing? He watched the man remove the helmet and was looking through the binoculars at the back of the man's head. Dark hair. Joseph's own hair on the back of his neck stood up. The biker finally turned his head to say something to the blond. Holy Fuck!! Silver Eyes!! He never thought he'd see him around here. Never thought he'd see him again anywhere! Joseph panicked. What does this mean? Does he know I'm here? How? Surely, I would have known if he'd been following me! His inner monologue was busy trying to figure out how this was possible. How could he and the partner of the dead cop be in the same place? The dead cop who Joseph had personally made sure was dead.

CHAPTER EIGHT

AS MURPHY and Justice stepped over the threshold of the cottage, Murphy's aunt hugged her tightly then turned to lay eyes on Justice.

"Aunt Ivy, this is Justice Coulter. Justice, this is my aunt, Ivy Mays." Justice held out his hand for a shake and Ivy placed her small delicate hand in his.

Ivy Mays was petite with salt and pepper hair that seemed to have a mind of its own. It was cut about three inches all over her head and stuck up in various places. She kind of had a punk rocker look to her. But what struck Justice most was her voice. It was not what you'd expect from such a petite woman. It was low and throaty and had a strength about it.

Since Justice wasn't really a big talker, Murphy was the first to break the silence. "How are you feeling, Auntie? When I spoke with you this morning, you didn't quite seem like yourself."

"Oh, for Heaven's sake, child, can't a woman have an off moment every now and then without you worrying about it?"

She was quick to add "Not that I'm not thrilled to see you, Dear, but I'm perfectly fine as you can see. And I'm very happy you brought such a handsome man with you!" Ivy and Murphy both turned towards Justice who didn't seem to be able to do anything other than blink back at them. Ivy hurriedly continued so Justice wouldn't realize they noticed his discomfort. "Can I get the two of you anything to eat or drink?" She turned towards the kitchen as though the question was completely rhetorical.

Justice finally found his voice. "Thank you, Ma'am, but we just had lunch at Katie's on the lake."

"Ah. How is Katie? It's been a few month's since I stopped in to see her. That woman sure can cook!"

Murphy was surprised to hear her aunt ask about Katie. She didn't realize they even knew each other but before she got the chance to question it, Ivy had gone into the kitchen to put a pot of coffee on and plate a few cookies, freshly baked from that morning she guessed by the lingering scent of cinnamon.

The little yellow cottage, Justice noticed, was not as small as he originally thought, and it also didn't look like a house belonging to someone he assumed was in her fifties. They were seated in the living room which held a large plump sofa. Two large modern wicker chairs flanked a fireplace and faced the sofa with what looked like an antique steamer trunk serving as a coffee table. The fireplace mantel was a bold piece of mahogany, stained just so it allowed the natural red in the wood to stand out. Curtains hung at the end of a beautiful bay window on one end of the room facing the road. A small writing desk with intricately carved legs was tucked away in the bay with an old wooden chair pulled out just enough to invite someone to sit. The other end of the room had an oversized archway cut from the wall which Justice assumed led to the kitchen. Opposite the fireplace was an open stairway leading to a second floor. Everything was modern but comfortable and Justice could see why Murphy loved it there.

Always on alert, Justice noticed no traffic went by as he was taking in the contents of the room. What caught his eye most though was behind one of the curtain panels. The butt of what looked to be a sawed-off shotgun was just out of place enough that he assumed Ivy had stashed it there when she heard them pull in. He could have assumed it was just to be used in case any forest critters got too close, but something else niggled at his brain... maybe some *other* critter was getting too close.

Justice was shaken from his thoughts as Ivy came in with a tray of cookies and coffee and sat beside Murphy on the sofa. "So, what are you two up to today, besides riding around making a hell of a racket?" Justice grinned at that and Murphy laughed out loud. They continued to chat and enjoy their coffee until it was time to go.

CHAPTER NINE

JOSEPH NEVER LEFT the window for fear he would miss seeing every movement from the little cottage. He had been wondering if the big man had a weakness. Hell yeah! A woman! He had seen her before. She often visited the older woman who lived there. He only paid attention for a couple of reasons. Number one, survival. He had to know what was happening around him at all times. Number two, boredom. Something he knew would destroy him if it continued.

But now if he could get rid of this person who could pin the murder on him, one out of two witnesses, he'd set out to find the other and could finally be free! Just the thought of freedom made his head spin. Now all he had to do was plan the big man's demise and he'd start that plan with the woman.

Movement brought his attention back to the cottage. He watched closely, eagerly, as the man and the woman donned helmets and positioned themselves back on the bike. But before starting the bike, the big man turned his head and looked directly at him. Joseph's head jerked back as though he had been punched! What the fuck? Could he see him? No fuckin' way! He brought the binoculars back up to his eyes just in time to see an evil grin cross the big man's face before he kick-started that massive engine and sped down Forest Road.

CHAPTER TEN

JUSTICE PULLED UP to Murphy's house in time to see Cassie walking up the porch stairs. She waved as he turned off the bike but continued up the stairs to wait on the porch swing. Murphy dismounted and took off the helmet to hand it to him. "Thank you for today. I really had a nice time and the motorcycle was surprisingly fun!"

He also removed his helmet after placing the one she had been wearing on the back of the bike. He didn't dismount though, and Murphy felt a bit of disappointment that he wasn't coming in, even though she hadn't invited him. His face was even with hers since he was sitting and she was standing beside the bike. His silver eyes found hers. "Can I see you again, sometime?" His voice was almost a growl and it settle low in her belly.

"Yes. I'd like that."

He reached out to put his hand on the back of her arm to draw her closer. His silver eyes lowered to her lips and he gently placed his lips on hers. Oh yeah. She forgot everything at that moment. Forgot where she was, what she was doing, forgot Cassie was waiting for her, couldn't even remember her own name! Just wow! His lips were warm and soft and... wait!... where'd he go? She opened her eyes when she felt the loss of heat and he was looking at her, studying her. "I'll see you, Wells." With that, he kick-started his machine, pulled his helmet on and, with one last long look at her, pulled onto the road and drove like a bat out of hell up the street.

Murphy stood there looking after him and didn't feel any time pass until she heard Cassie's voice next to her. "Hey! You coming in or you just gonna stand here with your mouth hanging open all day?" Geez. She hadn't realized she was standing there with her mouth hanging open but, yep!, there she was and it was open.

"Just making sure he got on the road ok. You know, just..." She trailed off knowing Cassie wasn't buying any of it. She looked up at Cassie who had her trademark shit-eating grin on her face. "Don't even say it!" Murphy said. "I saw you at the Raven's Claw last night making goo goo eyes at Richey Rich so just...don't!"

"Yeah?" Cassie stated as Murphy turned to go up the walk into the house. "At least I didn't start out calling the guy an asshat!" They both cracked up as they walked into Murphy's living room. Murphy rented the little house on Barberry Street. It was comfortable and close enough to The Joyful

Café that she could walk if she wanted to. When the weather was good, she did so often.

"Speaking of Richey, I mean Riley, you know I have to stop calling him that. I'm afraid I'm gonna call him that to his face! Anyway, how's it going with the two of you?" Murphy waggled her eyebrows for effect.

Cassie blushed a bit. With her fair skin and red hair, it was hard for her to hide what she was feeling. It usually came out full force on her face. "As a matter of fact, it's going pretty well. We're going to dinner tonight and I asked him to pick me up here. I didn't think you'd mind. I just was too nervous to sit around my apartment waiting by myself."

Hmmm. Maybe now was the time Murphy could get some answers. "Don't mind at all. In fact, invite him in. I'd like to get to know this man a little. And now, maybe you have a little time for a glass of wine?"

"I could really use one. I'm a bit nervous." Cassie bit down on her bottom lip as if to prove the point.

"Really, Cass? The formidable Cassie Thompson? The one all men drool over? The one who makes sure all men drool over her? Nervous? What gives?"

"Here's the thing, Murph." Cassie put her plump ass up on a kitchen bar stool, elbows on the bar then folded her arms and lay her head in them. She moaned. "Ugh. He's handsome. He's nice. He's rich. He's got a great apartment, a penthouse, for fuck's sake! A great car. A great job."

"Wow, maybe you really should dump him. He sounds like such a loser."

Sarcasm. Yeah, she got it. "Is he just too good to be true? I mean does this guy have any flaws?"

Murphy pretended to think really hard. "Let's see. Flaws. Yes. We're now looking for flaws. Hmmm. Maybe, just maybe, he's bad in bed! Would that make you happy?"

Cassie raised her head from the cradle she had made with her arms and frowned. "He's not." Then that frown turned into the biggest, most sinful grin in the history of grins.

Murphy had opened a nice bottle of merlot and set two glasses on the bar. At Cassie's last statement, she stopped, gaped at her, shook her head and poured the wine. Speechless. Yep. Nothing to say.

Annnnd saved by the bell. The doorbell rang and Cassie went to answer it as Murphy pulled down another wine glass and poured. They were taking a long time to come in it seemed, so Murphy peeked around the corner to her front door and found Riley and Cassie in one hot, smokin' lip lock!

Murphy cleared her throat. "Ahem. Would you two like to be alone?"

Cassie, the incurable smartass replied, "Thanks, Murph. I hate to kick you out of your own house, but if you insist."

Riley smiled that killer smile of his and looking at Murphy, said "Sorry, Murphy. I got a little distracted." He looked at Cassie. "Well, maybe more than a little. Anyway, great little house, you have here!"

Murphy handed Riley a glass of wine and motioned for them to have seats at the kitchen bar. She leaned against the counter. Riley wasted no time in questioning her. "So, went out with the big guy today, did ya?"

Before Murphy could answer, Cassie piped up. "She sure did! They didn't get home till after I was already here! Pulled up on that bad-ass bike and Murphy dismounted like an old pro!" Cassie giggled. Riley smiled. Murphy frowned at her.

It's not like I was driving the damn thing! Anyway, Riley, yes. Justice and I spent a wonderful day riding along the lake. We had lunch at Katie's then stopped to check on my aunt on Forest Road." Riley tensed at the mention of Forest Road. Before Murphy could be sure, he relaxed. She wondered if she had imagined it. "As a matter of fact, there was something I forgot to ask Justice. Maybe you could clear it up for me." One little white lie wouldn't hurt, would it? "What does he do for a living?"

Riley seemed to still which didn't jive with his regular MO at all. He was normally all smiles, loose, open, but now? A little stiff. "You didn't ask him?"

"Ah...no. I-I didn't get a chance." What? You expected her to be honest about being distracted by those lips? "What I do know is that he used to live in the area. Then he was gone for a while. I don't know how long and now he's back. I don't know what took him away or even where he went. You guys have been friends for a long time so I figured maybe you were friends before he left and you'd know all about him, yeah?"

Riley was still doing an imitation of stiff guy. He stared off into space for a minute, then blinked and shook his head just slightly. Seemed to bring him back around when that dazzling smile reappeared. "Well, yeah, Justice and I go back to grade school actually. Best friends through South Side High School. We even enlisted together. For any other information on him, I think you should ask him. It's not my story to tell." With that, he finished his glass of wine, thanked Murphy for her hospitality and turned to go. Taking Cassie by the elbow, he led her out of the house and into that fancy sports car of his, leaving Murphy to wonder what the hell?

CHAPTER ELEVEN

MONDAY MORNING CAME and since Murphy kept The Joyful Café closed on Mondays, she puttered around the house doing odds and ends and basically just killing time. She felt a bit lost. A bit empty. A bit lonely. Wow! She had no idea where these feelings were coming from. Or maybe she did. After just a couple of days of seeing Justice, the big galoot had wormed his way into her heart and she was missing him. Actually, missing him! Ugh! She finished some laundry from the day before then pulled out the book that, just a couple of days ago, she was dying to start reading. She opened it and read the first page. Realizing her mind had wandered and she had no idea what she'd just read, she read it again. Nope! No idea. Well, forget that. Hmmm. Maybe she'd go for a walk. Get rid of some of the pent-up energy. She pulled on a coat and boots, grabbed her keys and cell and took off down the street. She walked aimlessly for a while until she found herself in front of The Joyful Café. She stopped on the sidewalk and looked at the building. She'd have to decorate for Christmas soon. She stood there for a while and designed it in her mind and soon found herself caught up in picturing pine roping, white lights and large ornaments. A bit understated but warm and welcoming. Just what she wanted.

She jumped a little when her cell pinged telling her she had a text.

Justice – 'Hungry?'

Murphy pictured the edges of his mouth pulling up when she replied 'Always.'

Justice – 'How bout I pick up a pizza and come by?'

Murphy – 'Yum!'

Justice – 'Topping requests?'

Murphy – 'Whatever you like will be fine. Not picky about pizza toppings.'

Justice – 'About an hour?'

Murphy – 'Perfect. C u then.'

She walked home with a little extra bounce in her step knowing she would see him soon. When she got there, she freshened up a bit, just in time to hear the doorbell. She realized she hadn't heard his bike and when she opened the door, saw a truck instead. "No bike?" she asked as she motioned him inside. The smell of the pizza wafting up to her nose made her mouth water and she realized she hadn't eaten anything all day.

Justice looked good enough to eat. He wore the same biker boots, soft, worn jeans and his trademark black leather jacket. He set the pizza on the kitchen bar along with a six pack of beer. He took off his jacket and hung it on the back of one of the bar stools and Oh. My. God. He wore a white t-shirt that stretched tight across his massive chest. She realized then that she had never seen him without his jacket on. He had tattoos marking both arms in a bad boy fashion. Some kind of tribal markings maybe. She wasn't sure. Her mouth was watering and she stared until she heard him clear his throat. She looked up into his face and knew she was licking her lips. "Uh, what? Did you say something?" she managed to croak. Had he asked a question?

He grinned that panty-dropping grin of his and said "It's harder to carry the pizza on the bike."

She looked at him and drew her eyebrows down like she was trying to figure out what the hell he was talking about.

"You asked about why I wasn't riding the bike. Pizza and beer. Harder to carry on the bike." He was leaning back against the bar and crossed his arms over his chest making his biceps pop.

Murphy had to drag her eyes away from his body before she made a complete fool of herself and climbed him like a tree. "Oh yeah. I just never saw you without your bike before." And with that said, she needed to get her mind out of the gutter so continued "Pizza smells delicious. I haven't eaten anything yet today. I was actually out for a walk when I got your text. I was standing in front of my store, designing some Christmas decorations in my head. I know... eye roll, right? But, it will be here before we know it so I'm going to need to get started on that soon. I'd like to have it done right after Thanksgiving. Speaking of which, do you have family in the area you spend the holidays with?"

"No." Grumpy man was back with that one word. Geez!

"Ooooookay. Moving on then. So, Riley was telling me you were in the service together. Actually, scratch that. What he said was you guys were childhood friends who enlisted the same day. Did you both go into the same branch?"

Justice looked like he wanted to run. What was up with this guy? His brows lowered further than Murphy had ever seen them and he glared at her until she felt *she* might like to run. "Justice? Uh...are you ok? You look kind of explosive."

Justice struggled to get his feelings under control. Normally he'd just tell anyone being nosy to mind their own fucking business but this was not just anyone. This was Murphy and she was looking at him with those large, innocent eyes. Trusting. Yeah. That was the look. Trusting. Fuck! How could he expect her to trust him when he couldn't tell her the truth? At least not yet. And he felt more for her than he'd felt for anyone in a long time. He didn't want to lie but at the same time, he didn't want to scare her off. He would try to stall. "Why do you want to know?"

Murphy narrowed her eyes and drew her bottom lip in between her teeth. She studied the floor for several seconds. "Well, I thought if we're going to hang out together that, maybe we should get to know each other a bit and I was curious as to what you do – you know, for a living. I know you've been away for a while and wanted to know what brought you back. I was just wondering..." she trailed off as she noticed Justice staring at her mouth with an odd look on his face. Was that interest? Lust? Anger? Was he even listening to her?

When Justice realized she had stopped talking he knew he'd been caught but damn! When she pulled that lush bottom lip in, he couldn't think... at least not with his brain. His dick was thinking, though. Thinking about things it had no business thinking... especially when he couldn't be honest with her about his past or even his present. "Riley needs to learn to keep his mouth shut." Justice was growling but Murphy was quick to defend his friend. "He didn't really tell me anything. Just what I said and then he said the rest was your story to tell. And he didn't volunteer this formation. I asked."

"Why?" Damn! Justice was the one-word king!

"I told you why. Listen, Justice, if you're doing something illegal or immoral, I think I should know if we're going to …." Murphy stopped short when she realized what she was about to say. Instead she said "be…friends."

Justice's smile was pure devil as he pushed off the kitchen bar and took a step towards Murphy. "Is that what we're going to be? Friends?"

"Uh…well…" Murphy was stammering. What the hell? She wasn't a stammerer! She didn't even know if that was a word! She was definitely looking like a deer caught in headlights.

Justice took another step closer. One more and he would be directly in front of her. "Is that what you want, Wells? To be friends? Or do you want something more?" He took that final step and she could suddenly feel his heat – both from his body and his gaze but she didn't move. She couldn't and didn't want to even if she could. She wanted him. More than she'd wanted anything. He couldn't be a bad man, right? She'd sense it, wouldn't she? She was a good judge of character. That's why she was still single. Oh well, that thought wasn't very comforting.

Justice lifted his left hand and placed it on the side of her face. His eyes slid down from hers to her mouth. Then he lowered his head and pressed his lips to hers. Just a little pressure. Just a little taste. Just a little....

Murphy's toes curled and she felt her panties moisten. He was one hell of a kisser! Justice was having a hard time holding back. He reminded himself this was Murphy, not just a one and done. Even that had been awhile. Recently it'd been him and his hand. Speaking of which, he placed his right hand at the small of Murphy's back and pulled her close to him. With the feel of her flush against him, he turned his head a bit to deepen the kiss.

Murphy opened her mouth enough to let Justin in. His tongue was moist and sweet and tasted of mint and Justice...all man. She could feel the length of him, hard and hot at her belly and she couldn't hold back a moan. Justice took this as a good sign and rocked into her. He then pulled back, breaking the kiss and looked down at her. He had this overwhelming feeling of never wanting to let her go, of never getting tired of looking at her face and it scared the shit out of him! In fact, that thought had him taking a step back. He immediately missed her mouth and her warmth. "Sorry. I should've asked before I..." He left the words hanging in the air. All Murphy could do was blink at him.

They stood for what felt like an eternity when Justice's low voice broke the silence. "We should probably eat. You said you haven't eaten all day." Oh sure...like that was why she was suddenly light headed. Like it had nothing to do with that panty-melting kiss! She tried to smile but it came out more like a grimace until her eyes traveled down his large body and – holy shit! – she hadn't imagined it! He was long and hard and straining against the buttons of his jeans to the point she thought a button might fly off and put someone's eye out! Then her smile broke through! Knowing Justice was watching her, she thought, just maybe, he might be a little self- conscious, a little embarrassed. Boy, was she wrong! "Like what you see, Wells?" Oh. My. God! Just because the answer to that would be a resounding YES!, didn't mean he had to be so cocky!

"Just was thinking you might pop a button there, slick!" She laughed at her own joke and Justice grinned. "You're right though, we should eat before the pizza gets completely cold." She gathered plates and napkins and he picked up the pizza and a couple beers and followed her into the living room. She sat on the couch leaving room for him to sit next to her and they spread everything out on the coffee table. The pizza was still warm and smelled heavenly. She took a bite while Justice opened the beers. Setting hers in front of her, he took a long draw from his bottle, then picked up a slice and took a giant bite.

"So, ok, we never finished our conversation in the kitchen. Are you going to tell me what it is that you do?" Murphy asked.

God, Justice thought this woman was like a dog with a bone. And he was sure that the look on his face told her exactly that. "I do what needs to be done, Wells. It's nothing illegal or immoral if that's what you're worried about. That's about all I can tell you. Don't push this." He saw the hurt in her eyes just for a moment and felt bad that he had caused it, so he added, "Please."

"Ok, Justice. I'll trust you. For now." And that was that. She knew she wasn't going to get any information out of him tonight so she would trust. She would trust that she did have good enough instincts to know that he was one of the good guys. It was a feeling. It was the way he carried himself, so self-assured, so confident. Yet, he wasn't quite so cocky that he didn't let his emotions occasionally show through, even if it was for just an instant.

They talked and laughed while they finished the pizza and drank a couple of beers each. He had asked how her aunt was and started her telling stories of when she was little and spending time there in that little cottage. It seemed Murphy's mother worked a lot and her aunt played a large part in raising her. Justice loved watching Murphy when she talked about Ivy. He could see the passion on her face, the love, the laughter and he wondered if she knew about the weapon behind the curtain. "As a matter of fact," Murphy was saying, "I'm going to Ivy's for dinner tomorrow after I close the café. You wouldn't care to join me, would you?" She suddenly felt a little shy about asking.

"Does that mean you want me to go or you don't?" Justice asked.

"Sorry. I guess that was a weird way to ask. Yes, I want you to go. Would you like to?"

"Yes, Wells. I would like to go." This was exactly what he wanted to do. He needed to find out if the man he was looking for was really the man living on Forest Road. And if that meant he got to spend more time with Murphy...even better.

CHAPTER TWELVE

THE NEXT MORNING, Murphy woke early and headed in to The Joyful Café. She always arrived early enough to meet the baker who delivered the delectable treats she sold. His name was Jeff and he was always on time and cheerful. She guessed you would have to be a morning person if you were going to be a baker. They always took a moment to chat and fill each other in on what was in store for them that day. Today was no different than any other and after their chat, he was off again. She took her time placing the sweets in a sparkling glass case and making sure the café was ready to open. She moved among the tables and chairs, polishing here and there, even though there was no need. She took a lot of pride in what she had made. She hadn't unlocked the door yet when she heard someone knock softly. Glancing at the clock, she saw it was only five thirty. She normally didn't open until six. Someone's in a hurry this morning, she thought. Going to the door, she saw a large shadow behind the leaded glass. Justice! Opening the door wide with a smile on her face to match, he stood grinning down at her. His large frame filled the doorway and her heart filled her chest. "You're an early bird, this morning!" She said as she ushered him in to the café.

"I hope it's ok. I know you don't open for another half hour but I thought maybe I could get a coffee to go and I wanted to see you." The words tumbled out of Justice's mouth before he could stop them. "It's kinda nice to start out the day looking at something so fresh and pretty."

She was straightening some pastries in the case and thought Justice was talking about them until she looked up and he was lasered in on her! "Oh! Thank you." Murphy didn't blush often but when she did, she felt it clear up into her hair! "What can I get you?" And she knew as soon as the words were out of her mouth...

The devil was in Justice's eyes again! He grinned that evil grin that had her wishing he was against her, over her, under her, just somewhere close to her! And there was that blush again. Fuck! She couldn't help it! Justice gave a low chuckle which caused a rumble of her own deep in her belly. She really wanted this man! "Do you really need to ask me? I thought I was fairly transparent." He gave that same low chuckle, stirring up those damned butterflies in her...again. "For now, though, I'll have some coffee, black, in a to-go cup and be on my way." He winked at her and she was done! Stick a fork in her...done! She moved on jelly legs to make his coffee and set it on the counter in front of him. He laid money on the counter. "No charge." She said. "Then consider it a tip!" he countered, left the money, and walked out the door.

That man's gonna be the end of me, she thought. "I wouldn't mind if a man that looked like that would be the end of me!" Murphy jumped at the sound of Ava's voice. Ava worked part-time at The Joyful Café and Murphy hadn't heard her slip in the back door.

"I didn't realize I'd said that out loud." Murphy confessed. "But, yeah, he sure is nice to look at, isn't he?"

"Looks to me like he feels the same about you. Been seeing him long?" Ava had been with Murphy since she opened the cafe and had become a good friend and competent employee. She had semi-retired shortly before the opening of the café and was only wanting part-time so the arrangement was a win-win situation for both of them.

"Too long and not long enough. Does that make any sense to you?"

"Yep. He's gotten under your skin in too short of time, huh? Gotcha thinking about the possibilities?"

That's one of the things Murphy loved about Ava. She got it! She got *her*! "Maybe." Murphy said while thinking hell yeah, that's exactly it!

Murphy unlocked the door and turned the closed sign to open then turned around to survey her little kingdom. She grinned at the thought. Queen of her domain. Everything looked good and ready for the day.

CHAPTER THIRTEEN

THE FIRST TINKLE OF THE BELL above the door brought in Mr. O'Brien. "Good morning, Murphy, my dear. Isn't it a beautiful morning?" She adored Mr. O'Brien. In his 80's (at least), he was the perfect grandfather material. Too bad he wasn't much younger, she'd play matchmaker for her aunt.

"Good morning to you, too, Mr. O'Brien! Yes, it's lovely this morning. Crisp and fall-like. Your usual table is waiting for you and I'll bring over your coffee right away!" Murphy turned to get his usual but stopped when he spoke again.

"Would you happen to have any of those tasty blueberry tarts?" He was already licking his lips which made Murphy laugh out loud.

"Of course! And, guess what? I put aside one just for you on the house!"

He chuckled, gave her a quick wink and scurried over to his table, where he did what he did every morning...spread out the newspaper and quickly found the finance page. Murphy didn't know for sure but she suspected the sweet old man had made himself a small fortune during his working days and was living off the interest now. She brought his coffee and tart, gave his shoulder a quick squeeze and hurried off to help Ava deal with the line forming at the counter. She never lost money giving him treats on the house because when she did that, he just doubled his tip. Life was good!

After the morning rush, Murphy was wiping down the table tops when the bell tinkled letting her know there was a customer. In walked a man she had never seen before. He wasn't a large man, maybe about five feet seven, with sharp features, including a hawk-like nose that looked like it had been broken a time or two. Even though she didn't get the impression he was even in his forties, he had a receding hairline which definitely needed a good trimming. She occasionally saw a stranger in her cafe but this one made the hair on the back of her neck stand up.

He stepped through the doorway of The Joyful Café and let his beady eyes roam around the room until they fell on Murphy. *The blond.* That's the one. So close, he could taste the freedom. He couldn't help the seedy smile that crossed his face, showing crooked, yellowed teeth.

Murphy took a step back before she caught herself and forced a smile of her own. What the hell? She never reacted to people like this. She didn't like it, either. What if this was a sweet man and she was treating him like some kind of criminal? No. She didn't like this one bit. She forced a smile onto her face and tried to sound normal. "Good morning! Welcome. Please have a seat and I'll be with you in just a moment. Coffee?"

The man stared never letting that creepy smile leave his face. Then he seemed to realize she had spoken to him. When he spoke, his voice was high and had a nails-on-chalk board quality. "Yesss. Coffee would be nice." His voice had a hissing quality to it making the yes drawn out. He made his way to a table close to the door and sat so he could keep an eye on the door and out the window...and on Murphy.

She went about getting his coffee and brought the cup to his table. "Lovely day today. Would you like a pastry to go with your coffee this morning?"

He stared at her again. She wondered if maybe he was hard of hearing. "No. No passstry."

"Haven't seen you in here before. Are you new in town? Murphy was trying with all her might to be nice to the man but she was feeling creepier by the minute. She felt a bit better when Ava came in from the back room to add pastries to the glass case. Ava looked up when she heard Murphy's question. She could feel Murphy's... fear?... anxiety? she wasn't exactly sure what, but something was off. She took her time arranging pastries and wiping down counters so she could keep an ear on the exchange. Somehow, she knew Murphy wanted her there.

"Hope to ssstay if I can take care of a couple problemsss first." His words may have been innocent but his demeanor wasn't. Murphy had had enough. She wished him luck with that and walked behind the counter to Ava. Ava caught her eye and raised her eyebrows in a silent 'what the fuck' motion. Murphy returned the sentiment with a slight shrug and they busied themselves while the stranger finished his coffee. When he got down from the tall chair, he walked over to the counter to pay his tab.

"What kind of hoursss do you keep around thisss place?" He asked. Murphy thought about this for a minute and didn't really want to encourage him to come back but, since the hours were posted on the door, she couldn't very well not tell him. So, she told him when they opened every morning and left it at that. He gave a nod and headed out the door. She couldn't help but notice he checked the hours posted on the door, turned and gave her one last eerie glare and let the door close behind him.

"What the fuck was that about?" It was amazing to Murphy that Ava could voice the very words in Murphy's head.

"Whatever it was, I feel like I need a shower!" she shivered as Ava did the same. "I hope he doesn't become a regular. I don't think I could take that every day! Ew!" They both laughed a little uncomfortably and busied themselves with getting things ready for the lunch crowd.

When Murphy said goodbye to the last customer of the day walking them to the door, Justice was standing on the sidewalk talking to a man Murphy had never seen before. Must be the day for strangers she thought. Justice smiled when he saw her so she walked out to let him know she still had a few things to take care of before she'd be ready to go. Before Justice could introduce her to his friend, the man held out his hand and said "Hello, pretty lady. Where have you been all my life?" Murphy giggled a little but, before she could put her hand in his, Justice snarled – now this was a noise Murphy had never heard him make before – and pulled her to his side. His friend looked at Justice, then Murphy, who was looking at Justice, too, then back at Justice. "So that's how it is, huh?"

Justice snarled and glared at his friend. "Murphy Wells, Carter Stringer, a.k.a. Phantom. Phantom, Ms. Wells, owner of The Joyful Café."

Phantom made sure he kept his hands to himself this time but smiled all the same. "Nice to meet you, Ms. Wells. You are still a very pretty lady. If Striker ever gives you any trouble, let me know and we'll continue our initial conversation." He added a wink just to piss Justice off.

"Striker?" Murphy asked Phantom while turned towards Justice with raised eyebrows.

"Nickname from time in the service. We all had them so it's kinda a hard habit to break. Speaking of which, how's Wildman? Haven't seen him around lately. Still wild?" Phantom was now addressing Justice.

Justice looked uncomfortable but said "Not sure for how long. He's hangin' with Ms. Wells' best friend, Cassie Thompson, so I haven't seen much of him, either." Before anything else could be said or Murphy could raise one of her many question, Justice told her to go ahead and finish up what she needed to and he'd be in soon.

Murphy turned to walk back in to her café shaking her head and thinking of the nicknames. She'd just heard more from Phantom in five minutes about Justice's past then Justice had told her in as many days!

"Great timing." Murphy said as Justice walked through the door. "I'm just now finished." They walked out to the truck. She had walked to work this morning, knowing Justice would pick her up at the café and he had brought the truck instead of the bike due to the weather growing colder.

Murphy had called her aunt last night after Justice had left her place to make sure it was ok to bring him to dinner tonight. Not only was it ok, but Ivy had been positively thrilled. She said it would be good for both of them to have all that testosterone in the house again. She said it made a woman feel alive! Murphy had laughed out loud at that, and hid a smile remembering it now.

After they were seated in the truck, Murphy couldn't help herself. She turned towards Justice and grinned. He noticed and rolled his eyes. With a slight moan, he said "Ok. Out with it!"

"Striker?" She didn't say another word. She didn't have to.

Justice moaned yet again. "I knew you wouldn't be able to let that go. Phantom! Damn bigmouth!" He sighed. "Those who serve together have to have each other's backs so we all become close. Like family. We watch each other win and sometimes lose." He hesitated on his last word, a painful look taking over his handsome face, as though an unwanted memory had slipped through. "Just like brothers, we find nicknames that suit each other. Mine was Striker."

"Why?"

"They said I was like a snake. Always coiled and ready to strike." This was said simply, without hesitation, like it was no big deal.

Murphy didn't quite know what to make of his man. On the one hand, he was secretive about his past but this? This was something he said as though it was the most common thing in the world. "Phantom?" Murphy asked.

"Never see him comin! He just appears." Justice smiled. "There's something else I should tell you. Phantom, the smartass that he is, told me I should let you in a bit. He said he knew I wouldn't be telling you anything and that, if I cared for you at all, I needed to start talking or else I would just chase you away." Murphy's eyes were round and her mouth was hanging open. Justice chuckled and put a hand under her chin to close her mouth. "We agreed there are things I can let you know, without betraying anyone or anything. So...I was or *am*, part of a special ops group. Riley told you we enlisted the same day. We went into the Armed Forces. We both made it into spec ops where we met Phantom. After serving our required time, Phantom and I still work but that's something I'm not quite ready to share. You have to trust me on that one. Riley, or Wildman as we named him, opted to get out and make his millions managing bands. He has helped us out a time or two and will still do so whenever he's needed."

This gave Murphy an awful lot to think about. This was more than he'd ever said before. She'd need time to process it. So, she grabbed at the first benign thing she could think of. "Wildman? What's that about? Cassie may want to know!" Now it was her turn to chuckle.

"You've met Riley. It shouldn't come as a surprise that he likes the ladies. When we would have a mission that required getting info from a woman, no matter how tough that woman was, no matter how many people tried to get that info, Riley would just step in and poof! He'd have it without any problems at all. No interrogation. No bloodshed. None of the normal bullshit. He never really would tell us what it was all about, but we guessed. Women never could resist him!" He noticed that Murphy had a strange look on her face and knew what she was thinking. "Now before you go getting' all righteous and worried about Cassie, I've seen Riley with his share of women, and Cassie is not the norm. Honey, I think Riley has met his match in that one." This seemed to take care of her concerns because her face relaxed and she smiled at him. So, he continued. "Now, I know that's not everything but it's what I can give for now. You all right with it?"

"It's a lot to process but thank you. Thank you for sharing some of yourself. I'll have to remember to thank Phantom next time I see him, too." Justice growled and pulled onto Forest Road to head to Ivy's cottage.

CHAPTER FOURTEEN

JOSEPH TUCKER PACED in his grandfather's old house. Each passing day made him feel like he was losing his mind a piece at a time. He stopped at the window and stared at the little yellow cottage several times during his pacing. When he felt he just couldn't stand it anymore, he grabbed his jacket and headed out the back door into the chilly autumn air. He needed to clear his head and make his plans. He wasn't going to last long the way he was going. It was bad before but it had gotten much worse since he had gone into The Joyful Café. He just couldn't figure out how to get the girl to hand over fucking Justice Coulter without causing too much of a scene. He could sneak over to the cottage when she came to visit and force her to call him but that would include the woman who lived there. He didn't want to involve anyone else if he could help it. He was still pacing but now he was doing it outside, when he heard a motor. Not a loud one like the day with the motorcycle, but a softer one. During his pacing, he had ended up towards the forest butted up to the back of his grandfather's property, a good bit away from his back door. He stood perfectly still for a moment until he saw a pick-up truck pull into the driveway of the cottage. He didn't have his binoculars on him but there was no mistaking the large man who exited the truck's cab with a blond who was opening the passenger door. He tried to be inconspicuous as he walked back through the yard towards his door. He hoped he wouldn't be seen.

Justice and Murphy climbed out of the truck when Murphy noticed movement in the backyard of the old house next door. Even though it wasn't directly next door that's how she'd always thought of the place because her aunt and the old man who had lived there had been friends so sometimes she would play in the spacious lot between the houses. When she saw the man walking through the yard, her senses started tingling. She stared as he disappeared into the house. Justice noticed she had stopped and followed her gaze but was too late to see anyone. All he could see now was Murphy's pale face.

"You ok, Wells? Come on. Let's get you inside. You're not looking so good." Justice wrapped his arm around Murphy's waist and maneuvered her inside. Ivy opened the door and, without a word, motioned for Justice to set her on the couch.

"What happened?" Ivy demanded.

Justice never took his eyes off Murphy. "Wells? What did you see out there?"

Murphy's eyes finally met Justice's. Then she looked up to where Ivy was standing. "I-I'm sorry. It's just that there was this man who came into the café today and he was really creepy, and Ava and I felt dirty after he left, and..." Murphy knew she was rambling but couldn't seem to get a grip on herself.

Justice reached up and placed her soft, blond hair behind her ear. "Just take a deep breath. You're ok. Now, start at the beginning." Ivy ran into the kitchen to put on a kettle for tea and was back in an instant, lowering herself onto the couch beside Murphy.

Murphy recounted the incident with the man at the café today, letting Justice and Ivy know just how creeped out she and Ava both had been. "I'm probably just overreacting. But I've never had a reaction like I did today to any of my customers. It was as though this man was the devil himself. Pure, unadulterated evil. I would have dismissed it if Ava hadn't felt it, too. She was in the back room when he first came in then she stayed up front with me after she came out and saw what was going on. She said she could feel my discomfort and then she could feel his...intent would be the best word I could come up with at this time." She hesitated, taking a deep breath and accepting the cup of tea Ivy placed in her hand. "Anyway, I had forgotten about it with all our talking, Justice, so it came as quite a shock when I saw him in the backyard next door."

"Are you sure it was the same man?" Justice had walked over to the window to stare across at the yard. Yes, he knew it was him. What he hadn't known is that he had tracked Murphy. He was working hard to keep his anger down when all he wanted was to go over there and bash the fucker's head in. He'd kill him for his partner then he'd kill him again for fucking with his woman!

"I'm sure." Murphy said, jogging Justice out of his daydream. "He has an unmistakable walk. Almost like his leg had been broken and never set properly." Yes, Justice thought, that would be him. He remembered Phantom kicking that leg to bring the bastard down. He remembered the sound of the bone cracking in two. Then he remembered the sonofabitch rolling into a storm sewer along the curb. The opening was too small for either Phantom or Justice to go through and the mother fucker had gotten away. Until now.

CHAPTER FIFTEEN

FOR MURPHY'S SAKE, Ivy put on a smile and served up dinner as normal. She had outdone herself because she knew Justice was coming and she just had a feeling about him and Murphy. She felt he may become more than a mere friend. But, there was another feeling about him, too. One she'd like to explore. One that she had to do in private. There was definitely something more to this particular man. Something familiar. Something dangerous.

Justice and Murphy were seated at the table while Ivy served up a fork-tender roast beef, mashed potatoes with homemade beef gravy, candied carrots and a salad made with the most tender greens she could find. They all ate while they made small talk about the upcoming holidays.

"Do you have family in the area that you're seeing during the holidays, Justice?" Ivy asked. Murphy wasn't sure where she was going with this line of questioning, but she was hoping she'd do more since she, herself, couldn't seem to get direct answers. "Because I'm thinking Murphy and I usually spend Thanksgiving here at the cottage and there's always so much more food than the two of us can eat. We'd love it if you would join us for the day." Way to go, Aunt Ivy! Right to the man's stomach. And if how he's gulping down the roast beef today is an indication, it was as though she went for the jugular!

"Ivy, as long as it's ok with Murphy," he looked over and Murphy smiled and nodded her head, "then there's no place I'd rather be than right here with the two of you. Thank you."

Hmmm. Murphy realized he still never answered anything personal about his family! Geez! He was infuriating sometimes. But she'd forgive him because he was so nice to look at. She swore he realized he got away with not revealing anything when she caught his sly smile. Just a little upturn of the outsides of his mouth. And oh, that mouth....

"Save room for dessert. I've made something special!" Ivy rose from the table and disappeared into the kitchen only to return seconds later with the most delectable looking cake Murphy had ever seen! It had four layers and each layer was a different flavor starting with chocolate on the bottom, then a red velvet layer, coffee and cream came next and ending with the most wonderful ginger spice cake layer on top. Add to that whipped cream icing and fresh berries lining the top and wow! Ivy certainly had made something special! Murphy looked over at Justice and she swore he was almost drooling! So, food really was one of the ways to this man's heart? She intended to see if she could find another way later ...after they were home. *Yes!*

"Ivy, you're spoiling me. I haven't eaten this much since I don't know when and whenever it was, it certainly was not this good!" Murphy loved how Justice treated her aunt and she noticed how much Ivy enjoyed his company, too. Of course, it wasn't every day in Murphy's life that she brought someone to dinner. In fact, she hadn't since that boy in high school. What was his name? Oh, yeah. Bobby Fletcher. Lost her virginity to Bobby Fletcher. Typical boy/girl high school story. Boy meets girl. Girl thinks she's in love. Sex in the back of his car. Prom. Sex in the back of his car again. Summer. Broken heart. Well that about sums it up, doesn't it?

After what was the most delicious cake Murphy had ever eaten, she and Justice stood in the kitchen and did the dishes side by side. Ivy tried to object, saying she would get to them later, but it was the least they could do after she fed them such a delicious meal. This is what's normal, Justice thought. A family meal, then clean up in the kitchen, laughter, happiness. Love. Wait. *Love?* What? Where the hell did that come from? Justice never experienced this as a child. He really had never even experienced it as an adult. Most of his dinners were eaten on the run or a burger grabbed with his buddies in a bar. This, well, this was...what was this? He was lost in his thoughts, half listening to Murphy and Ivy chatter away. This was something he could get used to.

Dinner was done and the kitchen was cleaned when they took their coffee cups into the living room. "So, Ivy, tell me about this man living in the house across the vacant lot." Justice saw this as his opportunity to get a little more information.

Ivy hesitated, obviously thinking of where to start. "That house belonged to Paul Bates. He was a sweet, gentle man who had lived there as long as I can remember. In fact, when Murphy was a child, she would play in the yard between our houses and sometimes Paul would call her over and give her some little trinket he had bought just for her. Remember that, Dear?" Murphy smiled and nodded. "Paul was my friend and I miss him. He died last spring. Massive heart attack, they said. I had just seen him the day before. We had tea outside since the weather had warmed a bit." Ivy closed her eyes as though remembering that day with her friend. She opened them again and sighed. "But you asked about the man there now, didn't you? He appeared about a month ago. He almost never comes out of the house, and the house itself is almost in total darkness. I can occasionally see the glow of a small lamp or the flicker of the television. Nothing more. It's almost as though he doesn't want to be seen. I respect people's privacy but, after he was here for more than a week, I saw him, um, pacing I guess, yeah, that would be the word for it, pacing around the backyard. So, I figured here's my chance. I went out my back door and over to his. He evidently didn't see me approach so the shock on his face was evident when he finally noticed me standing there. Murphy's right. There is something disturbing when you look into that man's eyes." She drifted off again as though recalling that very day.

"Did he speak to you?" Justice asked.

"Yes. I guess you could call it that. He kind of hissed at me. It's as though he has a bit of a lisp but not. His speech is hard to explain but I can tell you I've never heard anything like it before and I'll never forget it. I said hello and introduced myself. He was to the point telling me Paul was his grandfather and he would be staying in the house for a while. He made a point of telling me he was a loner and didn't like nosy neighbors. I got his message loud and clear and left feeling, how'd you put it, Murphy Dear, creepy?"

Justice thought this over. It all made sense. No one knew he had a grandfather since no one claimed to be related to the evil bastard, so he thought he could hide out here unnoticed.

Murphy excused herself to go to the ladies' room and Ivy saw her chance. "Justice, I didn't want to say anything around my niece, but I know you are more than meets the eye. I'd like to know just what that is."

Justice looked stunned at first but hid that emotion immediately. Ivy was a clever woman who didn't miss much and she had seen it.

"It's in the way you are constantly watchful. The way you carry yourself. I know special ops when I see it, Justice. I'm no fool. I was in love with a spec ops soldier when I was much younger and now I know them when I see them." Ivy stared at Justice, defying him to deny it.

Justice didn't want to lie to Ivy. He wouldn't. "I told Murphy today that's what I was. Or am. I guess, once a spec op, always one. You're an interesting woman, Ivy, and I know you're tough, but I'm a bit worried about you being close to the man next door." Murphy had come out of the bathroom but paused in the hallway and listened in to their conversation. Justice continued. "I haven't told Murphy everything but I know that man, and you are both right. He is pure evil. I've been tracking him for the last six months until I found him here."

With that, Murphy flew around the corner and pierced Justice with her eyes. Anger and hurt swirled through her that he would keep something like this from her. A dangerous man living this close to her aunt? And he hadn't bothered mentioning it to her? What the fuck! "What the fuck, Justice!" Her mouth had gone dry and she was having a hard time swallowing. "Why are you sitting here talking so nonchalantly with Ivy when you knew she was in danger with some lunatic living right next door! And you didn't even say anything!"

Justice stood up. His large presence would have been intimidating if Murphy wasn't so angry. "Now just a damn minute! Ivy is not in any danger! This man doesn't want to draw any attention to himself whatsoever. In fact, I'm shocked that he even came into your cafe. Now, just sit down and let me tell you the whole story." Murphy never moved. She had been standing close enough to him that she had to look up when he stood. "Please." He added.

They stared at each other for several seconds. Then Murphy turned and, with a huff, sat beside Ivy on the sofa and crossed her arms.

Justice took a deep breath and began. He told them the sordid story of Leroy Bates. He began as a juvenile petty thief, fell in with some big-time gangsters doing some of their grunt work, worked himself up to one of the 'family'. Wanted out. Not for any reasons of redemption, but because the weasel thought he could be bigger and badder and get more on his own. Not the way it works. So, he faked his own death, had some plastic surgery and became Joseph Tucker. Started dealing in human trafficking. Not just any human trafficking, either. Kids. Boys and girls, average ages four through nine. Had his own 'company', if that's what you want to call it. Had his employees, but the sadistic bastard liked to do a lot of the work on his own. He'd steal these innocent children right out from under the parent's noses. Justice paused for just a second then continued. "One of the major flaws in this plan was that he likes to brag. His bragging is what alerted us. There were three of us who worked tightly together, bringing in Wildman, uh, Riley, as needed. There was Phantom, me and Professor. Tucker had to be taken down so we set him up. Found him online in one of those dark chat rooms where you went only if you knew where to look. We lured him out but the greasy sonofabitch got away." Justice paused again as though remembering something almost too painful to speak of. "Not before he took a slice out of the middle of Professor's abdomen. We tried to stop the bleeding but the cut was too deep. At least Phantom got a good kick in and broke the fucker's leg before he rolled away down a storm sewer drain. We tracked him here and we don't intend to let him go this time."

They were all quiet for a minute. Murphy had forgotten her anger, knowing Justice would never put either her aunt or herself in danger. Ivy was the one to break the silence. "I knew in my heart that number one, there was something not at all right about that man, and number two, that you, Justice, are more than what you seem. Now, how can I help?"

Murphy's intake of breath was audible, but Justice spoke before she could. "ivy, the only thing I want from you is for you to stay out of it. Don't think for a moment that I didn't notice that sawed off shotgun you keep around here. Don't try to play the hero."

Ok, now it was Murphy's turn. "What? What sawed off shotgun? What's he talking about, Ivy?"

"Just cool your heels, young lady! Just because I'm a mature woman doesn't make me old and delicate! I can shoot the eye out of a crow at a hundred and fifty feet when it's in flight! And I'm proud of the fact that I can hold my own. And, don't argue with me now, either one of you, but I intend to help if you'll let me."

Justice stared at the woman. Not his usual glare, Murphy thought, but just a thoughtful stare. Was he actually considering bringing her aunt in on this? Who the hell were these people, sitting in the living room talking about taking someone out like it's an everyday occurrence?

"I'd really rather you stay out of it, Ivy, but I'll tell you what you could do. Phantom and I need a place to keep an eye on Tucker. Your house would be perfect. Hide in plain sight, so to speak."

"Yes." Ivy said with no hesitation. Just one word and a nod of Justice's head and it was settled.

Murphy felt like she'd stepped into the twilight zone.

CHAPTER SIXTEEN

THEY LEFT THE COTTAGE after Justice made plans to bring Phantom by the next day. Murphy was quiet on the way home and Justice reached over to take her hand. She warmed at his touch and smiled up at him. "What you do...what you're doing...I guess it makes me nervous."

He nodded. "I get it, Wells, but like you said, it is what I do, and this one has gotten personal. Professor was a decent man. Someone I admired. Yeah...this is real personal."

They rode the rest of the way in silence but he kept her hand in his, occasionally rubbing his thumb across her palm. He pulled in front of her house and got out. She watched his big frame saunter around the front of the truck and stop to open the door for her to get out. He offered his hand again and she was lost to him. He held on tight to her as they walked on to her porch and unlocked the door.

They no sooner were in the house when Justice's hands came up to frame Murphy's face. He kicked the door shut behind him and lowered his head until his lips met hers. His tongue touched her bottom lip and she opened to him.

Glorious! The kiss went from soft to simmering to erotic within seconds. He walked her backwards till he had her pinned against the hallway wall. As his mouth did things so sensual she couldn't think, his hands moved down to her waist and pulled her into him, enough that she could feel his thickness through both their jeans. His hard ridge against her softness. "Murphy" he whispered against her ear. The way he said it was a plea. He never called her by her first name. It was almost a prayer. When a moan escaped her, he pushed her coat off her shoulders and let it drop to the floor, then quickly shed his own. He moved his lips from her ear down her throat, wickedly nuzzling, grazing, his beard stubble prickly but so sensual she wanted to feel it everywhere. He moved his hands from her waist but kept her pinned to the wall with his large body. He wanted to make sure she was constantly aware of his erection. No problem there! With one swift movement, he pulled her sweater over her head and it landed on the floor next to her coat. Then he gaped at her. "You're even more beautiful than I imagined." His tone was low making moisture pool between her legs. He reached around and put his hands on her ass, lifting her. Her legs automatically wrapped themselves around his waist as he carried her into the kitchen and set her on the counter. *Yes!* He knew it would be the perfect height. He undid the clasp of her bra with one hand while his mouth kissed and sucked its way from her neck to her nipple. His warm tongue lavished it until she thought she couldn't take it any longer. Then he bit down with his teeth, just enough to have her panting. He pulled away blowing gently where his teeth had been. The cooling sensation she experienced had her grinding herself on the counter. He watched her as he pulled off her boots and undid the zipper of her jeans. He raised her a little from the counter. "Pull your pants down for me." He'd get no argument from her! She hurriedly did as he demanded and he pulled back to look at her. She felt positively shameless sitting on her kitchen counter top in just a small scrap of lace panties. Red. His new favorite color.

He stepped between her legs and, wrapping an arm around her waist, pulled her to the edge of the counter. Her body slid forward easily, placing her center in direct contact with his. Even fully dressed, he could feel her heat. He let his lips meet hers again. Not so gentle this time, he took and she gave. Sliding his hand down, he ran his finger alongside the lace at the leg of her panties. She scooted closer, wanting him to go faster. He moved the fabric aside and ran his finger along her opening. Damn! She was so wet for him!

"Take your clothes off." She whispered, tugging on what she came to know was his signature tight t-shirt.

"Not yet. I want to last a bit, and the way you make me feel, just a look could set me off." His finger slid to that little nub of nerves at the top of her sex and she gasped! Wow, Justice had never seen anything more beautiful than Murphy, almost naked with her head thrown back and her mouth open. It was enough to have him coming in his jeans. But he wasn't a horny teenager anymore and he'd learned to control himself a bit better than that. A bit...hence, the clothes still on.

As his thumb remained at her clit, he slipped a large finger inside her, then two. She bucked up into him and he curled his finger just so and hit that perfect spot. That's all it took. She exploded! He kissed her. Hard. Swallowing her moans of pleasure. Working her until she stilled completely, then went limp.

He was watching her when she finally opened her eyes. A blush arose on her cheeks. A little late to be bashful now, she thought. She looked into those silver eyes of his and knew she still wanted him. She reached for the bottom of his t-shirt but he did that man thing and reached one hand behind his head, yanking it off with one pull, exposing his sculpted, broad chest. *Fuck!* She busied herself popping open the button fly of his jeans. Reaching in, she gasped again. *Fuuuuck!* He was huge! The head of his cocked popped up above his boxers. What a thing of beauty! Thick, hard, steel with a covering so soft she found herself petting it. The head was large and round and had a drop of pre-cum at the top. She bent to draw that precious drop onto her tongue, but he placed a hand on her shoulder to stop her. "Later, Darlin'. I won't last a minute if you do that right now." With that, he toed off his boots and pulled his jeans and boxers down at the same time. Kicking them to the side, he stood there in all his naked glory! Wow! Just...Wow! It all started with thick black hair and silver eyes, then broad shoulders, six pack abs, tapered waist. But what she really couldn't take her eyes off of at this moment was his arousal. Just the length of him made her feel heady, feral. He was so hard his cock was almost vertical. Standing there naked, just letting her look her fill was the most erotic thing she'd ever experienced.

He bent down to grab his jeans and pulled three condoms from his wallet, tossing them onto the counter. He saw her eyes go to the packets and smiled. "Awfully sure of yourself, aren't you, big man?" Murphy gave a shy little smile and looked at him from under her lashes.

"Yes." Annnnd we were back to the one-word king.

He stepped between her legs again and lifted her just enough off the counter that he could grab one side of her panties and pull them down those long lean legs. Now it was his turn to take her in. Keerist! How was he supposed to think when she was almost completely shaved? All she had was a little strip of hair right above her clit. That, along with the dew left from her first orgasm, was magnificent. Passion gripped his very soul and it was his turn to moan. He lowered his lips to hers and kissed her gently but she was having none of it. She threw her arms around his neck and pulled him in to her, then lowered her hand to place the head of his cock to her already wet entrance. He hesitated and she gave a little sigh of frustration, but he motioned to the condoms. Tearing a package open with his teeth, he rolled it down the length of his shaft. She was wondering if they sold them in XXXL. That thought flew right out of her head when he palmed himself and paused at her opening.

Meeting her eyes, he ran the head of his cock through her wetness, then shoved in just the tip. She gasped as he slowly...so very slowly...slid his length into her. When he was fully seated, he didn't move, giving her time to adjust to him. When she started to grind into him, he started to move. Gently until she wanted more. "Harder." He was realizing that Murphy wasn't one to hold back with what she wanted. He put his arms under her knees and raised her legs, setting her feet on the edge of the counter, all the while moving faster, grinding into her. Oh. My. God! This was deeper than anything she'd ever felt!

"Come for me again, Murphy." She didn't know his voice could get any deeper, sexier, but boy, she was wrong. That voice, this position and...Murphy cried out her satisfaction rather loudly. Her moans and his movements had him falling over the edge at the same time with a howl of approval of his own. He leaned into her and stayed there for a while with his chin on her shoulder, both panting, both sated.

Shifting a bit, he leaned his forehead against hers. After standing there a moment, not wanting to leave her warmth, he finally pulled out. She missed him already. She motioned toward the bathroom where he got rid of the condom. When he walked back into the kitchen, he found Murphy wrapped in a full-length flannel robe complete with fuzzy slippers. He watched as she poured water into a kettle for tea. He watched her for a while. Her movements were efficient and he occasionally saw a flash of leg when she bent a certain way. Yep! He was screwed! Drowning in the fact he could watch this for the rest of his life! A noise must have arisen from his throat because Murphy jumped a little, startled from her own thoughts. She turned towards him and her chin fell to the floor. This man definitely did not have a shy bone in his body. There he was, all six foot plus of him, perfectly male, perfectly naked, leaning against the door frame looking at her with...what was that look...part lust sprinkled with a bit of humor and a very large dose of heat? It was like a recipe for sex! He pushed off the door jamb and stalked her in full swagger. She couldn't resist this man even if she wanted to. And she did not want to. His eyes ran over her body and sparkled with devilish delight. "You're freakin' adorable, Wells."

She couldn't help but smile at that. How could he find her adorable in a flannel robe and fuzzy slippers? "Unlike you, I was cold." She winked.

Justice was full of surprises. "How do you know I'm not cold?" His turn to wink.

"Just how do you walk around with that tree between your legs?" This was fun.

He laughed out loud. A big booming sound, making her laugh, too. "Tree, huh?"

"Yeah. It's like a friggin' oak!" She licked her lips and drew the bottom one in between her teeth. Oh yeah, she saw what she was doing to him. She yelped when one arm went under her knees, the other at her back, and her feet left the floor.

"Bedroom." Said the king of one words.

"Last door down the hall...but wait! I need to turn off the tea kettle." He walked over to the stove and lowered her down just enough so she could reach the off switch and grab the other two condom packets. Then she was being carried through the hallway and quite literally, tossed on to the bed. She bounced just once until his body covered hers, large, imposing, and oh, so perfect!

"Three condoms, remember, Wells?" He still had that devilish look in his eyes as he lowered his head and met her lips. This man...her man...sure knew how to kiss! Wait! What? Her brain just registered what she had thought. *Her man?* She most definitely couldn't be thinking that! Once he caught the man he was after, he'd be off on his next adventure – saving the world – and she'd be just a memory, if he thought of her at all. The only thing she knew for sure was that she would never forget him.

CHAPTER SEVENTEEN

HER ALARM RANG early the next morning and she struggled to reach it, thanks to a large, warm arm thrown over her waist. She wiggled out from underneath Justice's arm, turned off the alarm and got into the shower. She smiled as she got herself ready to go open the café. She would dismiss all thoughts of him eventually leaving because right now, life didn't get any better than this. After showering, she walked into her bedroom and stood, awestruck at what she saw. There was just enough light from the bathroom to see his magnificent form over flowing her queen-sized mattress. The quilt that had taken her months to make was pulled up to his waist leaving every ripple of that glorious back exposed. He still laid in the same position she'd left him in with one of his strong arms laying across where she had been. She took a minute just to take it all in, to keep the memory so she could visit it later.

"You're starin' at me, Wells." His voice rumbled deeply.

"You're worth staring at, Justice."

He chuckled and opened his eyes, as he raised up on one elbow and squinted at the bedside clock. Murphy watched as his muscles rippled. "It's still early. Why don't you get some more sleep?" she said. "There's bread for toast and orange juice and coffee if you want. Help yourself. Just lock up when you let yourself out."

"I have a better idea." His voice was raspy from sleep making it even deeper, sexier. She didn't think it was possible. "You come back to bed with me and we'll make good use of that last condom." They had worn themselves out after the last bout of mind bending sex last night and one lone condom was shining like a beacon from the top of her nightstand. Oh, what she wouldn't give to do just as he had asked but...

"As enticing as that is, I have to meet the baker in about twenty minutes so I have to go." God! He was leaning back in her bed looking at her, his silver eyes sparkling in the low light. He was absolutely beautiful!

"Well, then, how about I stop by the café for coffee after I shower and run a few errands?" While waiting for her answer, he threw back the covers and stood. He grinned when he heard her gasp. "I'd tell you it doesn't mean anything, that it's just morning wood, but we both know better." He winked as he strolled over to kiss the top of her head. "I'll kiss you properly after I use the facilities." He waggled his eyebrows as he continued past her to disappear into the bathroom.

She went into the kitchen to grab her things for the café then slipped into her coat. Justice appeared wearing only jeans slung low on his hips and wrapped his arms around her. Heat spread through her as he kissed her...properly, as promised. They said their goodbyes, and she was out the door and headed for the café.

CHAPTER EIGHTEEN

NOT LONG AFTER Jeff, the baker had gone, still early by most people's standards, the bell tinkled over the café's door and Ava looked up to see a tall, handsome man walk in. A stranger to the café, he looked around as though looking for someone. Not seeing them, his eyes settle on Ava. She smiled and asked if she could help him.

"I was hoping to find..." He never got to finish what he was going to say when Murphy came through the doors from the back. "Well, hello again, pretty lady." He smiled and Ava felt like she needed to fan herself. "I made sure Striker wasn't here before calling you that. Wouldn't want to rile him up this early in the morning, now would we?" He winked. Murphy looked in Ava's direction. Ok. It's official. Ava was having to hold on to the counter top. Inwardly, Murphy rolled her eyes.

"Phantom! Good to see you again! Ava, this is Phantom. He's a friend of Justice's. Phantom, this is Ava, my friend and employee extraordinaire." Murphy wasn't sure if Ava would be able to stand at all when Phantom turned that killer smile on her.

"I wasn't aware there were two pretty ladies here. You should put up a sign...give a man some warning!" His smile widened as he put a hand over his heart for dramatic effect.

Ava mumbled something but neither Murphy nor Phantom caught it. Murphy assumed it was because it was gibberish, all Ava could spit out at the moment. Ava glanced her way and Murphy raised a what-the-fuck eyebrow. Ava looked appropriately embarrassed while managing to put a sentence together and asked if she could get something for Phantom.

Phantom ordered a special coffee and told Murphy he was meeting Striker so she seated him in the back booth knowing their meeting would require privacy. She had just sat across from him to keep him company while he waited when Justice walked through the front door. Her breath hitched when she saw his form fill the doorway. He looked around until he caught her eye and smiled...then it turned into a grimace when his glance landed on Phantom. He made his way over to the booth and leaned in to give Murphy a kiss on the cheek. "Good morning...again." He turned to glare at Phantom who looked like the cat who ate the canary. Yep. Phantom seemed to be his own kind of king...king of the shit-eating grins. Justice leaned in. "Make a move on my woman and I'm gonna have to hurt you where it would hurt the most."

Phantom held up both hands, palms out in a surrender position and tried to keep that trademark grin from coming out. He almost made it. "Wouldn't even think about tryin' to cut in, big man. Anyway, this pretty lady is a bit young for me, I'd have to say." He winked at Murphy again.

Murphy thought about that as she slid from the booth. She hadn't really paid much attention to age, but now that she was looking, yes, she could see that, even though his clothes couldn't hide the tall, lean muscles that could belong to a much younger man, his face was a little more weathered, rugged. Yes, she got why Ava was still walking on jelly legs. His wink had told her he and Justice were just pulling each other's chains when she felt strong arms around her. The arms that had held her close all night. He kissed her again, a bit more passionately this time. The mood was broken when Phantom cleared his throat and raised one eyebrow at Justice.

Again, not a modest bone in the man's body. He let go of Murphy slowly, asked her for his favorite coffee blend and sat across from Phantom with a shit-eating grin of his own.

Phantom decided he liked the effect Murphy had on Striker. He deserved happiness after the negligence of his childhood and the horrors they both dealt with as adults. "Happiness looks good on you, my man."

Justice looked at the man who was like a brother to him. The man who'd taught Striker to survive in the worst situations he could imagine. "Maybe you want to give it a try sometime." Striker's remark had Phantom sitting back in the booth with a who me? look on his face. Striker continued. "Looks to me like Ava wouldn't mind giving you a whirl. She hasn't taken her eyes off you." He wasn't surprised Striker had noticed. The man never seemed to miss a thing. Phantom looked over to where Ava stood behind the counter. Ava, embarrassed at being caught, hurriedly gave her attention to the pastry case. "She is a pretty one. But, no zing, ya know?" Striker hadn't known what he meant when Phantom first told him about the infamous zing. It was the little zap of electricity a man felt when he first laid eyes on *the one.* He hadn't known then but he knew now. Murphy had him experiencing the zing even now every time he looked at her. "Anyway, I had that zing once. Not every man gets to experience even that much. I'm not expecting to have it again." Striker knew Phantom had been married. He also knew the rat bastards who had killed her. He knew them because he, Phantom, Professor and Wildman had made sure they'd gotten no less than they deserved. They wouldn't be hurting anyone ever again. He was watching Phantom's eyes, knowing he was remembering, too. Too bad ending someone didn't take away the pain of the living.

As though not wanting to dwell in the past, Phantom got down to business. "So, you said on the phone this morning, we have a place?"

Striker turned all business, too. "Right next to the fucker! Murphy's aunt, Ivy, lives on Forest Road. Their houses are separated by an empty lot, which Ivy also owns. We were having dinner there last night. Ivy confronted me when Murphy stepped out of the room. Said she knew I was special ops. Seems she was close to someone who was also in the business a long time ago. Close enough that she saw signs that most people wouldn't. We had been talking about the 'new neighbor' and she knew what I was after. Murphy heard us talking from the hall and jumped all over my shit! Thought I was using Ivy but Ivy jumped right back at her. Told her she was helping us in any way she could and there was nothing Murphy could do about it. There's probably some sort of back story there, but I don't know it. Anyway, I told her it sure would help if she'd let us use her house so we could get a bead on this guy. No hesitation whatsoever on her part and I don't think Murphy would have a chance against her!" He chuckled a bit, letting Phantom know that last part was said with respect on both parties. "I told Ivy we'd come over today, get the two of you acquainted, and go from there."

They drank their coffee and talked about different scenarios of how to take the bastard down with as little mess as possible. They knew he was a wild card and would try to kill anyone coming anywhere near. He had nothing to lose. And now, not only did they want to protect themselves and each other, they needed to protect Ivy and Murphy, too.

Justice promised Ivy he would text her when they were coming. So, they finished their coffee, he sent out the text and they piled into his truck, already filled with surveillance gear they would install. His text pinged almost immediately with the message that Ivy was making a trip to the grocer. She told him to just come in the way they'd planned and she'd see them in a little while.

Phantom and Striker pulled off Forest Road onto what was barely a path which led to a garage on the side of the cottage not facing where Joseph Tucker was hiding out. They would take that path as long as needed so he wouldn't be aware of the fact they were staking him out. Striker led Phantom into the cottage and they checked it out for locations where they could set up. There was a spare bedroom on the first floor on the side of the house facing Tucker. This was Ivy's craft room so there was already a large table and a couple chairs. She had moved all her supplies to a corner cupboard so everything would be out of their way. They unpacked their equipment and went to work setting up wireless cameras, monitors, video recorders and speakers. Headphones were also made available. Tonight, they would put a few microphones and cameras in and around the house he was holed up in. If they got lucky, he'd go out. If not, they'd improvise. They had discussed going in and just taking him out. They both liked the sound of that. However, they weren't cold blooded killers and the feds they had contracted with, asked nicely if they would bring him in alive. Yeah, right. Feds and asking nicely should never be used in the same sentence. But they would do what they could. That didn't mean, of course, that they wouldn't kill him where he stands if they had to.

They were just installing the last video camera when the key turned in the front door and Ivy entered with two bags of groceries. Striker appeared instantly and took the heavy bags from her. He turned to take the bags into the kitchen and she followed, removing her coat along the way. The video camera they were working on happened to be in the kitchen so Phantom was just cleaning up their tools. Striker, being Striker, took up the entire doorway as he walked in so Phantom didn't see the woman behind him until Striker put the groceries on the counter. Then Ivy looked at him and smiled. *Zing!!*

"You must be Phantom." Ivy said. "Justice told me about his partners. I'm sorry to hear about Professor. I'm sure it's a great loss."

Phantom just stood there a minute, staring without blinking. Striker raised his eyebrows then cleared his throat to snap his friend out of whatever the fuck that was. It worked. Somewhat. Phantom seemed aware that it was his turn to speak. "Um. Yea. A loss. Thank you." Yep. Genius on board. Christ! How was he going to do his job when he couldn't even complete a full sentence?

Luckily, Ivy didn't seem to notice. Maybe she thought his idiocy just came naturally. She turned to Striker. "Did you get along ok? Find everything you need?"

"Indeed, we did. Let me show you where we put everything." He gestured for her to go out of the kitchen first so he could turn to his friend. "What the fuck was that, man?" he whispered. Phantom swallowed hard and shrugged his shoulders.

Striker felt odd showing Ivy around her own house. She seemed impressed by the progress they'd made and he explained they were going to do some covert installation at Tucker's house after dark.

"I was going to make some dinner. You in?" Ivy asked.

"I'm gonna go see Murphy then I plan to come back after dark to do the install. Then, we'll start surveillance tonight.'

Ivy turned when Phantom walked in to where she and Striker were talking in the living room. "What about you, Phantom? I'm a decent cook. You in?"

Phantom was trying his best not to look dumbstruck. This woman was doing things to him that he hadn't felt in what felt like forever. "Uh. Yea-yes. Thanks." And the genius just keeps coming! Phantom's eyes flicked to Striker's, whose eyebrows had risen almost to his hairline. This was a

Phantom Striker had never seen before. He was usually calm, smooth, and when it came to the ladies, the epitome of suave. But this Phantom? Clumsy, tongue-tied and awkward.

Again, lucky for him, Ivy didn't give any indication that something was up. "I'm going to get things started then." With that, she headed into the kitchen.

Striker walked closer to Phantom. "What the hell is wrong with you, brother? I've never seen you act like this before. It's almost like you're seeing a woman for the first time!" He stopped speaking abruptly and started grinning that shit-eating grin. "Oh man! I got it!" He lowered his voice so Ivy wouldn't hear. "It's the zing, isn't it? That's what it is! It's the zing!"

Phantom's head fell forward and he slowly shook it from side to side. "Who would've thought I would ever feel the zing again? Shit. Shit. Shit!" He raised his head and looked into his friend's eyes. "Shit."

Justice was still chuckling when he went into the kitchen to let Ivy know he was leaving.

CHAPTER NINETEEN

MURPHY WAS JUST LOCKING UP when two strong arms came around her at the back door. She'd know those arms anywhere. "Hi" he said softly in her ear. "I've been waiting all day to see you. Instead, I had to look at Phantom's ugly mug all day."

Murphy giggled. Yes, giggled. "Ava didn't seem to think that way. Did you notice?"

"Hard not to. I thought you were going to have to strap a drool cup to her chin." They both laughed and Justice put his warm lips to hers as he turned her around. "So, what would you like to do for dinner?"

Murphy thought for a moment then suggested they pick up Chinese take-out. He agreed and said he'd get it and meet her at her house.

Less than an hour later, Murphy and Justice were relaxing in her living room with forks and take-out containers. Seemed they both felt the best way to eat Chinese was to share containers and neither one liked chopsticks. Could get more on a fork. Justice couldn't help but notice how comfortable this was...how much it felt like, what he assumed, family felt like. He knew he was moving fast but he'd never felt this way before. He liked to watch Murphy eat. She wasn't one for having a salad and nibbling on it like some of the women he'd known before. There was no pretense with her. She liked food and wasn't afraid to show it! He smiled at that when she looked up and caught him. "And what's funny?" she asked.

"just enjoying looking at you, Wells."

"So, you think I'm funny?" She crossed her eyes making him laugh out loud.

"I was just thinking how nice this is, sitting here with you, sharing our food."

"Ivy and I used to do this. When I was young, we'd sit in the living room on the floor around the coffee table and talk about our day while we shared our take-out. She cooked most of the time but sometimes we'd treat ourselves. It was nice, too, not having to do dishes, just throw out containers. Did your family ever do that?" She felt Justice tense. Uh-oh.

Annnnd the one-word king showed up. "No."

Murphy looked at him. Was that hurt in his eyes? Regret? She couldn't quite get a read on him at this moment. "Sorry,

Justice. I don't mean to pry. I guess I'm just trying to get to know you. You know, what you were like when you were younger. How you were raised. I'm sorry if I brought up bad memories."

Justice signed. "I'm the one who's sorry. I can't give you what you want at this time, Wells. I hope you understand." He looked into her eyes, willing her to do so.

"Now that's where you're wrong, Justice. You can most definitely give me what I want." She teased. She really did not want him to feel pressured by her. And, sitting close, sharing a meal, not only felt good. It felt right.

Justice stopped with a forkful of fried rice halfway to his mouth. "That sounds like a challenge, Wells."

"You up for the challenge?" she waggled her eyebrows. Yep. Giggling again.

Justice didn't even mutter an answer. He put the container down on the coffee table and was on her before she even finished her giggle. He tasted like Chinese food and she just could not get enough of him. He laid her on the floor without removing his lips from hers and laid beside her, bringing her leg up around him so she could feel his hardness. When he broke the kiss, they were both breathing heavy. Without speaking, he pulled her shirt over her head and, holy shit! A black lace bra dipped low between her breasts making them spill over. He licked his lips, then with one hand unhooked her bra, letting it fall onto the floor. His mouth went to her breast where he lavishly nipped her while undoing her jeans. After unzipping them, he grabbed the waistband and pulled them down and off. Fuuuuck! Black panties! His cock twitched and he knew he'd have zipper marks if he didn't get out of his own jeans. But first things first. He moved between Murphy's open legs and scooted down stopping when his mouth was in line with her center. He could feel her heat on his face and smell her arousal. He glanced up and found her watching him with that bottom lip sucked in between her teeth. She couldn't be any more beautiful than she was right now. He licked up her opening until he got to that precious little nub. He sucked on it while he let two fingers enter her and curve up a bit to hit just that right spot. She reached down and put her hands in his hair as she lifted to meet his fingering strokes. It wasn't long before she stilled then exploded. "Yes! Oh God!" Justice stayed with her like that till she was done and boneless. When he raised his head again, she wasn't looking at him this time. Her eyes were closed but there was a huge grin on her face and pink on her cheeks. He raised himself up and with one swift movement, had her turned over with her stomach on the floor. Putting his hands on her hips, he pulled her ass up so she was on her hands and knees. She heard a package being torn open. She looked over her shoulder in time to see him smooth the condom down over his hard shaft. That was a beautiful thing! He positioned himself behind her and pushed. He entered her in one stroke and she gasped. "Yes!"

He didn't fool around this time. He started grinding and moving in and out. The faster he went, the faster her breath was coming in gasps. He wasn't going there alone. Oh no. He reached down around her and found that nub again. Putting his thumb directly on it, he added some pressure and moved it in circles, as his hips moved in and out in rhythm. Annnnd....yes! Oh God! was definitely the words of the day!

CHAPTER TWENTY

AFTER STRIKER HAD WALKED out Ivy's door, Phantom didn't know what to do. Having his usual suave demeanor vanish made him feel uncertain. Oh. Hell. No. He didn't like it. Didn't like it one bit! He could hear Ivy rustling around in the kitchen and music was playing, too, but he couldn't seem to get his legs to move in that direction. So, it came as no surprise to him that he jumped when Ivy stuck her head out around the kitchen doorway.

"Sorry. I didn't mean to startle you. You must have been deep in thought. Well, when you're ready, come on in and sit. You can have a glass of wine or a beer and we can get to know each other while I throw dinner together." Phantom nodded, just once, so she'd know he'd heard her and Ivy disappeared back in to the kitchen. Infernal woman! Where does she get off making him feel this...this...whatever the fuck this was! Well, he'd just have to go in there and straighten this out! Yep! Just go in and...and...he ran both hands down his face, then through this hair. He found himself wishing they were her hands. Oh, come on! He didn't even know this woman so this must be purely physical. He could handle physical. He could handle it well. He relaxed a bit then remembered the zing! Shit! That zing wasn't just physical, not if the past had been correct, and he knew it had.

He pushed himself to walk into the kitchen. He made it to the doorway and stood there watching her. She was a petite, curvy woman and he liked what he saw. He didn't know how long he watched her. She had the radio playing on the counter and she was dancing. The hard rock was playing and the bass was booming and she was shaking that ass while she chopped vegetables! And what a sweet ass that was! Heart-shaped and encased in a tight pair of jeans!

Leaning on the door frame lost in the sight of Ivy dancing in the kitchen had his heart swelling with a feeling he barely recognized! Happiness sparkled inside him and he couldn't help himself. He was beside her in an instant shaking his own ass, matching her step for step.

She didn't even show surprise when Phantom started dancing beside her, she just threw her head back with laughter and shook it even more.

The song ended and Foreigner started crooning 'I've been waiting for a girl like you'. Phantom held a hand out as an invitation to Ivy and she stepped into his arms without hesitation. *Ziiiiing!* He wrapped a hand around her waist and kept her right hand in his left. She felt...perfect...like she'd been made just for him. They danced without speaking as he listened to the words, he wondered if he had been waiting for a girl like Ivy. Waiting for a chance to settle down. Waiting for happiness. When the song ended, she stepped from his embrace and laid a hand on his chest. "I haven't danced like that in a long time. Thank you, Phantom." Her voice was soft, womanly, and had a hint of melancholy. It struck him like an arrow straight through his heart.

"The pleasure was all mine." Wow! An entire sentence. Progress! "Now, what can I help you with?"

"I was just chopping some veggies for salad. If you'd like, you can finish that while I tend to the chicken."

He picked up the knife and started chopping green peppers as she pulled chicken from the oven, added some cheese and spices, and returned it to the oven so the cheese could melt. They chatted about the weather and made other small talk as the food was finished then they carried it to the table by the window. Phantom waited until Ivy was seated before seating himself.

Like the living room, the kitchen was cozy, comfortable. The table was surrounded on three sides by a built-in banquette covered in a soft plaid fabric with matching pillows in different patterns but similar colors. There was a hanging lamp with a large drum shade that would cast light onto the table when turned on but there was still enough light outside that Ivy hadn't turned it on yet. She had lit several candles and had turned on a small lamp on the counter, making it even cozier.

"It's a nice place you have here, Ivy. Lived here long?"

"Seems like forever. I bought this property about twenty-five years ago. I just wanted something I could call mine. Worked out well, even better when Murphy would stay."

"How did that come about? Where were her parents?" Somehow Phantom felt comfortable enough with Ivy to ask such a personal question.

"Her mother worked a lot. I'm not quite sure she ever got comfortable being a mother. Some people just aren't cut out for it, you know? Anyway, she was my sister and I loved her. And I loved Murphy. So, I was happy to have her spend most of her time here with me. Murphy was a wonderful child and has grown into an even better adult. Strong, smart, capable." Ivy's voice trailed off and she had a far-away look in her eyes. Remembering, no doubt.

"Looks like she had a great role model to me." Phantom's voice had dipped into that lower register, making him sound raw and sexy. This was not lost on Ivy.

"You wouldn't be flirting with me now, would you, Phantom?" Her mouth was turned up into a teasing smile.

"Would you mind if I was?"

Hmmm. She got a warm fuzzy feeling in her stomach. Even though men had always flirted with Ivy, it had been some time since she wanted flirt back. "I don't think I would mind at all." They both smiled, content to just sit and talk.

Phantom wanted to know about her. "Striker told me you confronted him, telling him you knew what he was." He laughed a bit as he told her the next part. "I think you blew him away a little bit. Not just that you were so forward, but that you were right!"

"I knew the minute I met him. You see, I was..." she hesitated, searching for what she wanted to tell. Funny, she felt she didn't have to hold anything back from the man sitting across from her. "...involved with a man who was special ops. I grew close to his friends, too. They taught me that you can learn a lot just be watching someone, that is if you want to know. And with Justice, I wanted to know."

"Because of his involvement with your niece." This was more of a statement than a question. Yeah. Phantom got that. Protect your own. If only he could have protected his...

"Phantom? Still with me?"

He looked at her, really seeing her, and not just his past. Ivy's eyes were large and the color of cognac, rich and deep.

He wanted to get lost in those eyes. He wanted to be done with the sordid life he was living. Sordid wasn't how he used to look at his life but now he wanted a simpler one. A house, peace and a woman. Not just any woman. Someone who would be a partner, who he could love and be loved by. He wanted *this* woman. The realization hit him hard as he looked into Ivy's eyes.

"Are you ok?" she asked, using that soft, womanly voice that could undo him.

He cleared his throat but it was still raspy when he spoke. "I'm as ok as I have a right to be."

"That sounds like you think you don't have a right to happiness."

He looked out the window towards the forest edging up to the property. "I've done some things I'm not proud of, Ivy." His voice was gruff. He continued when he brought his eyes back to hers. "And it looks like I'm not done."

"Do you want to be?" she asked simply.

"Yes." Just saying that one word loosened his shoulders a little. "I've never told anyone that before, not even Striker."

"I understand. Your profession seems to get into a person's very soul. It becomes who they are, not what they do. That would be hard to walk away from."

This woman would be hard to walk away from. "True, but I felt differently about it when I was younger. Now that I've got some age, I've found I want something...else." His eyes slid to what was outside the window again.

A moment passed and Ivy knew he would have let the conversation go, but she couldn't. "What is it you want, Phantom?"

His eyes were on the trees but he wasn't seeing them. He was seeing his life as something different. A house, a yard, a dog, a woman. His head turned slowly towards Ivy and his gaze locked on hers. *"This."*

His one word didn't surprise Ivy, although by the look on his face, she guessed he surprised the hell out of himself.

They sat in silence for a short while, each lost in their own worlds. She knew he was trying to work through his feelings and she was trying to let him. What he didn't know was what Ivy was feeling. From the moment she had laid eyes on him, she had soaked in his six feet plus frame, all sinewy, taut muscles, wide shoulders. The kind of body a man in his profession had to keep up and from the looks of him, he did a damn fine job of it. His hair was short, cut in a military style with some gray running through it, enough to make him look distinguished. Deep blue eyes, that sexy scruff on his chin. Oh yeah. He'd thrown her for a loop and she knew she'd thrown him for one, too.

There had been no one for Ivy since Keith. He was special ops, too. Brave. Noble. Faithful. An alpha male who lived hard and loved the same way. She had planned to marry him but he was killed before she got the chance. His team was rescuing teenage girls from human traffickers. The girls were being kept in a warehouse somewhere in Africa, waiting to be moved out the following day. It was the middle of the night when Keith and his team, after a four-day reconnaissance mission, went in through a rarely used back entrance only to be discovered after getting the next to the last girl out safe. Keith had gone in for the last girl when they had been ambushed. Neither made it out of the warehouse. His team wasn't even able to retrieve the bodies. The warehouse had been burned to the ground with the bodies inside. She hadn't met anyone all through these past twenty years who could stand up to her memories of Keith. Until now...

CHAPTER TWENTY-ONE

IT WAS STARTING to get dark outside and Justice had to return to Ivy's cottage soon. He and Murphy had finally gotten up off the living room floor and had their clothes back on. They were standing in the kitchen now and he put his arms around her waist, pulling her tight against him. "I have to get going. Phantom and I have some work we need to do tonight."

Murphy tried to hide the worry she was feeling but not doing a very good job of it. She never did quite figure out how to keep her emotions from showing on her face. Justice put a finger under her chin and raised it so she'd be forced to look at him. "What's this all about?" he asked.

"I can't help but worry. I don't really want Ivy caught up in this. She's just not cut out for this kind of thing." Murphy's arms spread out as though the motion would indicate the kind of thing she was referring to.

The corners of Justice's mouth tipped up slightly. "Uh...Honey, have you met Ivy?" he chuckled. "I know I haven't known her long at all, but that is one of the toughest women I've ever met and I've known some women in special ops who could cut a guy's balls off with just one look!" Murphy didn't look convinced so he tried again. "Murphy." He said in a softer tone. She was sitting up and taking notice now since he usually reserved calling her by her first name for when they were having sex. "Murphy." He said again. "I would never do anything to put Ivy in danger. Phantom and I have been working together for years. We know what we're doing. One of us will always be with her during this mission. Don't worry. Please."

"I'll try. That's all I can promise. I'm going to go spend some time with Cassie tonight. Riley is out of town working on something with the band so I told her we'd have some girl time. I haven't gotten to see much of her with Riley taking up her time and you taking up mine...not that I'm complaining." She gave him a wink and a big grin and kissed him quickly. Moving out from his grip, she grabbed her purse and made her way towards the door.

"Oh no you don't" he laughed, grabbing her around the waist. "You're not going anywhere after that sorry excuse for a kiss. You can leave after this." With that, he lowered his head to hers and kissed her lips like she was water and he was a man dying of thirst. He released her and the look in his eyes told her she just might be late to Cassie's.

She giggled and jumped from his reach. "If you keep this up, neither one of us will get to where we're going!" She reached the door and jerked it open and was on the porch before he could grab her again. He stepped out after her. Both of them laughing, they got in their cars and drove in opposite directions.

Murphy drove to Cassie's place and parked in the lot designated for the apartment building. She rang the buzzer for the third-floor apartment and Cassie's voice came through "Murph, is that you?"

Murphy laughed at Cassie's ever-present enthusiasm. "Yes. Let me in. It's getting cold out here." The door buzzed and Murphy walked through and up three flights of stairs. Cassie was standing at the top watching for Murphy to round the last flight. She made a little squeaking sound when she finally spotted her and ran down the last flight to grab her best friend and hug the stuffing out of her.

"I can't believe you're finally here! I feel like I haven't seen you in ages! Come on, I can't wait to catch up!"

"Oh my God, Cass!" Murphy said, trying to look pitiful but breaking out in a grin instead at her best friend's ramblings. "Why do you live on the third floor? Couldn't you have gotten something closer to the ground? Or, at least, something with an elevator?"

Cassie looked suddenly serious. "We do have the service elevator, if you ever want to use that." Murphy busted out in laughter, threw an arm around Cassie's shoulder and stomped up the last flight of stairs with her best friend at her side.

There was a bottle of wine and two glasses on the coffee table and Murphy removed her shoes and settled on the couch with her legs tucked under her. Cassie grabbed two platters from the kitchen counter and brought them to the coffee table, too. She was not the domestic goddess type but this was impressive. Three kinds of cheese, cut just so and at room temperature, grapes and a variety of stuffed olives were displayed in the middle, an assortment of crackers rimmed the large platter, and on a small platter, brie with plum jam and sliced almonds wrapped in filo dough and baked to golden goodness. Murphy eyed the platters, looked up at Cassie who was still standing, looking a little nervous. "Hmmm. Catered?" Murphy asked. Cassie's eyes widened a little and she shook her head. "You did all this?" Murphy's eyes widened a little, too. Cassie nodded and sat on the couch next to her friend. "Cass, since when can you do all this? Not that I didn't think you could, just you've never shown any interest. It looks delicious! And it's beautiful. Too bad we have to destroy it by eating it!" She laughed and Cassie seemed to blow out a breath she didn't know she was holding.

"Murphy. It's just unbelievable. I feel like a new person! Riley is amazing. He's taught me so much! I feel like I've been living selfishly, having everyone take care of me and feeling like I deserved it! He's opened my eyes to giving of myself instead of always just taking." As Cassie spoke, Murphy couldn't help but smile. She could see the happiness in Cassie's eyes and she could feel that Cassie wanted her to accept this change.

"Cass, I never felt you were selfish to begin with. You just weren't very domestic. So? There's nothing wrong with that. But I gotta tell you, if you insist on feeding me like this, well then, I guess I'll just have to be ok with that." They both laughed, happy to be in each other's company again. "So, tell me all about his superman that is Riley Harrison. I want to know about the man who is keeping my best friend happy."

"I don't even know where to start. He's smart, Murph. I mean scary smart! The way he handles business for the band is remarkable. They're gonna be big, like BIG! He doesn't take any shit and trust me, I've heard them try to dish it out, but he just shuts it down and moves on. Tough but fair, ya know? And then there's his looks, well, you've seen him. Gorgeous!"

"Yea, but how is he in bed?" Murphy knew this would light Cassie up. She blushed a little. "Wait! What the hell! Are you *blushing?*" This was new for Cassie. She was usually the one making everyone else blush!

"I know. I know. The former party girl has met her match! Key word here being former! He's the one, Murph. I didn't think it was possible, but there he is...the one!"

Murphy studied her friend sitting there, looking as lovely as ever. Something was different about the *former* party girl and Murphy was looking for what it was. Ah! There it is...love. She'd seen Cassie in a lot of things before...lust, like, dislike, indifference, but never this. Never love. It looked good on her and Murphy was happy for her friend.

"What are you staring at? Do I have cracker in my teeth?" Cassie brought a hand up in front of her mouth as though she really did have something in her teeth. Murphy laughed.

"No. I was just thinking that I've never seen you in love before, and it looks good on you." She leaned over and gave her friend a hug. "I've missed seeing you, Cass, and I'm happy for you. I knew it would happen someday."

"And now it's your turn to spill. Come on. Let's have it. What's up with you and that hunky Justice? Is he still surly and king of the one-word sentence?"

"Yep." Murphy growled and paused long enough for Cassie to catch on to her one word. They both cracked up! "Actually, once we got past all that surliness, he's amazing, too! He's caring, smart, sexy, built like a brick house, did I mention sexy?"

"Yeah. I've seen him. Very sexy!"

"Hey! Keep your eyes on your own sexy man." Murphy laughed but her smile faded somewhat as she continued. "He's still a bit of an enigma though, Cass. He shuts down if I bring up his past. He won't discuss his family. In fact, I don't even know if he has a family. If I start asking questions, he returns to the king of the one-word status. It's weird."

"Is it that important to you? Do you feel you have to know about his past in order to go forward with your futures?"

"That's just it. I don't know."

"You don't feel like he's hiding something, do you?"

"No. Well, I don't know. I trust him completely. That doesn't make any sense, does it? There's something in his past that has hurt him. I can see it in his eyes before he shuts it down. I guess it just bothers me a bit that he won't share it." Murphy sat back into the couch and turned her face so she could look out the window. You couldn't see much because of the darkness and the fact that she was on the third friggin' floor, but she wasn't looking at anything in particular anyway. "I just think I might be falling for this man and I'm not sure what to do about it."

It was Cassie's turn to study Murphy. "Do you think he's feeling the same?"

Murphy shrugged her shoulders. "I don't know. We seem to want to spend a lot of time together. He shows up at the café when I least expect it. I've met his friends. Ivy is smitten in that way aunts get when they think a guy's perfect for their nieces. I guess I'll just have to wait and see."

"Hmmmm. So how is he in bed?" They cracked up again knowing that Cassie was throwing Murphy's words right back at her!

"Oh, don't think I'm gonna blush! I'll tell you straight out...he's large and in charge!" This time, they laughed so hard, they almost fell off the couch!

CHAPTER TWENTY-TWO

JUSTICE LEFT MURPHY'S and drove to Forest Road where he turned his truck onto the forgotten path and into Ivy's garage. He sat in the truck for a minute before going in to the cottage, thinking about Murphy. He wanted her. He had been reviewing his life lately and thought maybe he was ready to find someplace to settle and now that he had met her, he was thinking this just might be the place to do just that and give up this lifestyle that was sure to kill him sooner rather than later. He got out of the truck and entered the cottage, stepping into the kitchen. He spotted Phantom and Ivy sitting at her kitchen table. They seemed a little startled to see him.

"What the hell? Weren't you expecting me?"

Ivy was the one to respond. "Of course, we were expecting you. I guess we just lost track of time."

Justice raised an eyebrow at Phantom. Lost track of time, my ass. This had sexual tension written all over it. He stared at Phantom, waiting for him to say something. Phantom's eyebrows came down and he stared back at Striker, daring him to say something in front of Ivy.

Once again, Ivy acted oblivious to the tension between her new housemates and said "Justice, there's some chicken and salad left over. Are you hungry?"

"No. Murphy and I shared Chinese take-out. Now she's over visiting with Cassie. But thanks for the offer." Then he turned towards Phantom again. Ivy had gotten up to clear dishes, waving away Phantom's offer to help. Striker slid in to the seat Ivy had vacated. "So, what's happening with our target?"

Phantom looked towards the window again. "Not a movement. Not a sound. Seems like he doesn't want anyone to know he's even in there."

"Well, imagine that." Striker and Phantom headed for the surveillance room to pack up the items they'd need when they saw a shadowy figure in the front of Tucker's house. "Looks like he may be on the move, after all."

"One can only hope." They donned their night vision goggles and watched the wretched little man as he moved from his front door to the front of his garage.

CHAPTER TWENTY-THREE

JOSEPH TUCKER'S beady eyes squinted through the darkness towards the garage that sat by the old house. He had been watching the cottage but nothing seemed out of the ordinary. Same lights on as always. No cars in the driveway except the one belonging to the woman who lived there. He hadn't seen the blond girl or the large man for a few days, either. He had to get out for a while before he went stir crazy. Slowly opening the garage door, trying to make as little noise as possible, he got into his Chevy and turned the key. The car was dark gray, not too old, not too new. Nothing to draw attention to it or to himself. He slowly pressed on the gas pedal and drove without lights down the driveway and onto the street. He allowed himself to go a good quarter of a mile before turning on the lights, not sure if he just needed to drive or if he would find an out of the way bar to get himself a drink.

Phantom and Striker watched silently as Tucker drove away. Not believing their luck, they got to work immediately. Dressed all in black including black knit caps on their heads and eye black on their faces, they picked up the bag holding the surveillance equipment. Ivy had volunteered to keep an eye on the road for signs of Tucker's return and was hooked up with earphones and a mic so she could communicate with them should the need arise.

Stalking across the lot separating the two properties, they tried the back door thinking maybe he was just crazy enough to leave it unlocked. No such luck. Phantom was on his knees in an instant with his trusty lock pick and they had access in seconds.

After entering the house, they both reached down and activated tiny lights built into their shoes. They found this to be better than flashlights due to the fact the lights were lower and couldn't' be seen as well from the outside. They quickly located the window where Tucker would sit watching the cottage and installed a camera and microphone under the sill. They would be able to see and hear whatever happened in that room and he wouldn't be able to see the equipment unless he was specifically looking for it. They were hoping he talked to himself.

After arranging that one and making sure there wasn't any sign of them being there, they installed the same above the kitchen cabinets and alarms at the front and back doors. This would keep them aware of his movements in the house and let them know if he went in or out.

Satisfied with their work, they gathered their tools, turned off their shoe lights and crept back across the joining lot where they entered the cottage through the back door.

"Honey, we're home!" Phantom chuckled low in his throat at his own lousy imitation of Ricky Ricardo's accent. Striker stopped and turned towards his friend.

"Who the hell are you and what did you do with Phantom?"

Phantom laughed out loud as Ivy came around the corner. "I take it by the good mood that everything went as planned?"

"Yes, Ma'am." Phantom still had that shit-eating grin on his face and when Ivy looked at him, she put on one of her own.

Striker looked from one to the other, drew his eyebrows down, sighed loudly and walked out of the kitchen heading towards what was now known as the surveillance room. It seemed like everybody was getting hit by the zing! Riley, himself and now Phantom. Maybe there was something in the water. He donned headphones and picked up his cellphone to text Murphy while he waited.

Justice – 'Hey. Having a good time?' His phone pinged almost immediately putting a smile on his handsome face.

Murphy – 'Yes. Girl talk is good and so is the wine. In fact, I may crash on Cassie's couch tonight.'

Justice – 'Sounds like a plan. And I'll feel better knowing you're safe.'

Murphy – 'Awwww. So nice to know you care.'

Justice – 'You know I do.'

Murphy – 'I do, too.'

Justice – 'Have a good time. Text me in the morning when you get up.'

Murphy – 'Ok. Good night, Justice.'

Justice – 'Good night, Murphy.'

They wore identical sappy grins as they both shut off their phones.

Phantom appeared in the doorway with a mug of coffee in each hand and sat in the chair across from Striker. Striker removed his headphones before accepting the mug.

"Ivy went on up to bed. Said to tell you good night." Phantom sat back in the chair. "Has our friend returned?"

"No. So, you and Ivy, huh?" Striker looked at his friend. Phantom waited to see what he would see on Striker's face. Would he have to defend himself? But there was no judgment on his face or in his eyes, only curiosity.

"Looks that way. At least, I'm hoping."

Striker nodded once then said "why don't you get some sleep? I'll take first watch. I'll wake you in a few hours unless our boy does something interesting before then."

The cottage had a second bedroom which Ivy had made up for whichever man wasn't on watch. They also had set up a makeshift cot in the surveillance room in case they wanted to stay closer to the action. Striker talked Phantom into taking the bedroom so he moved up the stairs without making a sound. He paused just for a moment outside Ivy's bedroom. It's too soon, he told himself. Just keep walking. He forced his feet to move down the hall and into the spare room. A small lamp was lit on the bedside table and the bed was turned down. He used the attached bathroom then stripped down to his boxers. He didn't realize how tired he was until he laid back against the cool pillows and pulled up the sheets. The last thing he remembered was turning off the light and closing his eyes.

CHAPTER TWENTY-FOUR

MORNING CAME EARLY for Murphy. She woke up disoriented with a dry throat and a slight headache but the smell of strong coffee was already making her feel a bit better. Tumbling off the couch, she leaned on the kitchen doorway when Cassie handed her a large cup filled with the dark roast.

"Good morning, Murph." Cassie eyed her friend inspecting the disheveled hair, smeared mascara and lines from the couch pillows on one side of her face. "How are you feeling this morning?"

Murphy narrowed her eyes at Cassie. "Why are you so chipper this morning? You have a lot of nerve being up and looking that good this early, especially when I feel like dog shit that has been set on fire, stomped out and set on fire again!!"

Yikes! Cassie gave her a big grin. "I guess I can just handle my booze better than you." Murphy made some sort of a sound between a growl and a snort and headed toward the bathroom. "There's extra towels in the linen closet and I

put some of the extra clothes you leave here out for you, too."
They each made a habit of keeping some extra clothes at each
other's places just in case. She heard Murphy mumble
something but decided it was best that she didn't understand
it.

After her shower, Murphy was feeling better and headed
back to the kitchen where she joined Cassie at her center
island. "I just texted Justice. He's gonna pick me up for
breakfast. Invited you, too. You in?"

Cassie squinted at her. "Do you want me to be in? Or do
you want that sexy man all to yourself this morning?"

Murphy laughed. "Oh, my sides hurt. I haven't laughed
like we did last night for a while! And, yes, I want you in. I'll
get the sexy big man all to myself later." She waggled her
eyebrows.

Cassie rolled her eyes but couldn't help but smile. "Come
on, then. Let's not make him walk the stairs. We'll meet him
by the door."

They walked together down the stairs talking about
nothing, like only close friends could. Justice pulled up just
as they exited the apartment building. True to form, he got
out of the truck and opened the passenger door, shutting it
after making sure both ladies were in, then got in the driver's
side and gave Murphy a quick kiss. "Good morning, ladies.

Did you have a good time last night?" Both women talked at once assuring him that, indeed, a good time was had last night. They kept on talking, sometimes over each other as Justice just shook his head and pulled onto the street.

After she realized he wasn't headed into town, Murphy asked "and just where are you taking us this morning? This isn't the way into town."

"I thought we'd eat at Katie's on the lake today. If that's ok with the two of you."

Cassie didn't hesitate. "Oh! I haven't been there for a year or so! I'd love to go to Katie's! She is the best cook and her breakfasts are huge!"

Justice grinned, glancing over at Murphy who smiled back and said "I guess it's settled then. We're off to Katie's."

A short while later, they were seated at a table by the window while Katie herself was pouring coffee and making small talk. Murphy was watching her, admiring her. "Katie, I found out recently that know my aunt, Ivy Mays."

Katie paled for just a moment and stopped pouring coffee. It was as though time had stopped. She still held the pot in the air but just wasn't letting any slip out. She seemed to catch herself quickly and finished pouring. She turned to look at Murphy, really look at her. "Yes. Now that I'm looking for it, I definitely see family resemblance." She turned her gaze on Justice. "Have you met Ivy, Justice?"

He seemed slightly confused by her question. Then you could see the moment he got it. He gave a slight shake of his head as though to warn her off this line of questioning before answering. "Yeah. She's one great lady."

"How do you know her?" Murphy was curious before but now that she caught that weird exchange between Justice and Katie, she was even more so.

Katie glanced at Justice before continuing. "Ivy and I had friends in common when we were younger. She's a strong woman, that aunt of yours. A fine, strong woman. Now, I need to get back to the kitchen. What can I whip up for you folks today?"

Murphy knew her curiosity had been blown off and she told herself she'd find out from Justice when they were alone. The three of them placed their orders and Katie disappeared into the kitchen to cook.

They ate delicious omelets, pancakes, hash browns and toast while laughing and talking. Cassie filled Justice in on what Riley was up to since they hadn't seen each other for a while, and after everyone was caught up and had full bellies, they loaded themselves back into the truck and Justice drove them back to Cassie's apartment. After making plans to meet up with Murphy later, Justice headed back to the cottage.

"What the hell was that exchange between Justice and Katie when I asked about Ivy?" Murphy asked Cassie as they climbed the three floors to her apartment. "Oh, for Christ's sake, Cass, couldn't you find an apartment a little closer to Earth?"

Cassie gave Murphy a little smile. "Then how would I keep this fantastic ass in such good shape. These steps have a whole lot to do with it, ya know. And as for Justice and Katie, I didn't notice anything unusual."

Murphy just shook her head. "That's because you were drooling on the menu! Geez! It's like you haven't eaten in months!"

"I haven't eaten Katie's cooking in months! And that was some damn fine cooking!" They were both giggling all over again when they finally got to Cassie's apartment door.

CHAPTER TWENTY-FIVE

JUSTICE FOLLOWED his regular pattern as he traveled back to the cottage, turning onto the hidden lane and parking in Ivy's garage. Ivy was in the kitchen baking something that smelled delicious. She smiled up at him when he came through the door.

"Good morning, Justice. I didn't get a chance to see you before you hurried out the door to see my niece this morning. Did she and Cassie have a good time last night?"

Justice shook his head and grinned. "Those two...when I asked them that question, I'm not sure I even got an answer! They both started talking at once and never stopped till we got to the restaurant."

"That's them, all right. Thick as thieves!" They both laughed.

"I don't know what you're baking, Ivy, but it sure does smell good!"

"Glad you think so. I thought we could use some cookies to snack on so I'm making some peanut butter with chocolate chips and I just started a batch of oatmeal raisin."

Justice sniffed appreciatively. "Phantom in the surveillance room?" Ivy nodded and Justice headed in that direction. He stopped before reaching the kitchen's doorway. "Uh, Ivy?" She turned to see him looking at her with a look in his eyes she didn't quite recognize. "We went to Katie's this morning for breakfast." He hesitated but when she didn't say anything, he continued "Murphy mentioned that you and she were related. Uh...Katie's husband was on Keith's team, wasn't he?" Ivy had confided in Justice, telling him about Keith and how he was killed.

Ivy stopped mixing her cookie batter and gave Justice her undivided attention. "Yes. The two of them never really hit it off and I think she always felt a little guilty that her man survived when mine didn't. But I know it wasn't his fault. I know that team members have each other's backs no matter what." Her gaze dropped to the floor not really seeing what she was looking at. "Did she tell Murphy?"

"No. I stopped her. I'm not sure what Murphy knows about your past, but what she knows should come from you. No one else."

"Thank you, Justice." They stood in silence for just a moment then Ivy turned and began to mix the batter again and Justice left the room knowing that losing someone they loved, having them taken from this Earth in such a violent manner, was something Ivy and Phantom had in common.

Striker found Phantom in a chair in the surveillance room with a set of headphones dangling from one ear and his nose buried in a magazine. He looked up when Striker entered and nodded. "Our friend's been quiet today. No movement. No sound."

"Not much last night either. I watched him pull his car into the garage, saw on camera that he checked the cottage through his window, then he must have gone to bed. I figured, unless he does something out of the ordinary, we'll survey him till after Thanksgiving since that's only a couple days away. Unless this guy makes some sort of move, there's no reason to fuck up Ivy's Thanksgiving plans."

Phantom nodded. "Agreed. Plus, you get a large, home cooked meal," he said with mischief in his eyes. Before Striker had a chance to say anything, he continued. "Speaking of which, she invited me to Thanksgiving dinner, too." He arched an eyebrow in Striker's direction.

"Well, for all that's holy, man, don't keep me in suspense!" Striker fluttered his eyelashes and folded his hands under his chin in his best girly pose. "Are you dining with us or not?"

Phantom's eyebrows came down in the perfect v. "I'm not sure who you are anymore." He glared at Striker but couldn't stop the corners of his mouth curling up a bit when Striker gave him his best shit-eating grin.

Striker sat down in the chair opposite Phantom and sighed. "It'll be good to have a real Thanksgiving. Been a long time for both of us."

Phantom grunted his agreement knowing he and his friend were thinking of all the shitty ways they'd spent the holiday in the past, some in the trenches, some on missions, some eating nothing at all. Striker donned headphones and looked towards the house where Tucker was holed up. They sat in silence for a long while until Striker moved his headphones off one ear. "How do you see this going down? I can't see this guy wanting to run. He has it made here, compared to other places he's had to hole up in. Got a roof over his head, a car, and he doesn't know about us sitting right here hoping he'll fuck it all up."

Phantom thought about it. "I'm thinking we might have to take him. We'll see if he displays any type of pattern so we can set up our own ambush. I'm hoping the guy's as dumb as he looks but we both know you don't rise to the ranks with crime lords like he did by being dumb."

"And to fake his own death and have them believe it? He's either got brains or balls the size of Cleveland."

They fell back into silent companionship until Phantom removed his headphones and stood to stretch his legs. "Gonna see what's to eat and then catch some sleep. Wake me if you need me, brother."

Striker gave a thumbs-up and turned his eyes back on the house next door. Part of their stealth training had been to quiet their thoughts and he was unusually good at it, but not today. Today his mind kept drifting to a beautiful blond with blue eyes and a curvy ass and it was determined to stay there. He thought about the night they had spent together. How her eyes went dark, her lids went shaded. So fucking sexy! He could hear the little sounds she made then the full out moans. Before he knew it, his cock wouldn't stop thinking of her, either. It was straining uncomfortably against the zipper of his jeans and he shifted to adjust himself. He hadn't been this hard just thinking of someone since he'd been a teenager, but instead of fighting it, he wanted to give in and seize it. He just had to make sure he didn't move too fast. He didn't want to scare her off.

Phantom stalked into the kitchen where Ivy was washing the last cookie sheet. Two large platters of the sweet-smelling things sat on the counter looking like something out of a magazine. "Why don't you take a break and sit with me awhile? I wouldn't mind having a cup of coffee before I grab some sleep."

Ivy put the cookie sheet in the dish drainer and wiped her hands on a kitchen towel. She reached into the cupboard to get the mugs but Phantom was already opening the cupboard door. Their arms brushed as they both reached for the mugs. With his front to her back, she could feel his flat abs against her, his heat surrounding her. Then, instead of moving, he leaned into her a little, pushing her into the counter's edge. Her breath caught and that's all he needed to hear. He spun her around and had his lips on hers before she could even let out a gasp. He had turned her a little rougher than he had intended but she didn't seem to mind. She froze for only a moment then wrapped her arms around his neck, pulling him down. Oh. Yeah. He raised one hand and brought it to the side of her face while he tightened the other around her waist. He drew her closer and deepened the kiss, exploring her greedily with his tongue.

When he broke the kiss, they stared into each other's eyes, breathing heavily. She felt dizzy with want and desire. His blue eyes were almost navy and if she even thought she was mistaken about his intentions, he pressed her into him so she could feel his erection against her belly. Nope! No mistaking this!

Phantom's eyes searched her face as though hoping to read her thoughts. "I'd apologize if I was sorry, Ivy, but I'm not. No woman has made me feel like this since..." he hesitated briefly, hoping she didn't catch it, "well, for a long time."

It was Ivy's turn to search his face but it had gone blank with what he hadn't said. "What happened with her?" Ivy knew she shouldn't have pried when Phantom took a step back. She quickly reached out to put a hand on his forearm. "Phantom, I'm sorry. It's really none of my business."

Phantom's eyes were shaded. "It's a story for another day. I think right now I'm more tired than what I thought. I'm gonna skip the coffee and just go to bed." With that, he turned and strode from the kitchen, leaving Ivy feeling empty.

CHAPTER TWENTY-SIX

NEXT DOOR, Joseph Tucker was feeling more like a caged animal every day. Not that he hadn't spent time alone before. He had, but not like this. He'd never stayed holed up in the same place for this long and he'd always had the next job to look forward to. But this? He was lost, alone and feeling a little crazier, a little more reckless, with each passing day.

He was sitting in the same old chair he always sat in, staring at the cottage. There was something about that cottage, but he just couldn't put his finger on it. Something he should be seeing. Something. His senses had been tingling since he arrived, but after seeing the blond and her large friend, he'd been on high alert. The problem was he had nowhere else to go. He was tired of skulking around in seedy hotel rooms and alleyways so he wouldn't be seen. This was the best place he'd found and he sure as hell wasn't going to let some lowlife fucker scare him away from it! He'd just stay alert and keep watching.

CHAPTER TWENTY-SEVEN

IVY FINISHED CLEANING the kitchen, poured two cups of coffee and took them in to the surveillance room. There she found Striker with his headphones on, staring out the window deep in thought. "I thought you might like some coffee" she said as she placed the steaming mug on the table beside him.

He removed his headphones and flipped the little switch that would sound an alarm if Tucker left the house by either door. "Ivy, you were reading my mind." Striker smiled but when Ivy tried to smile back, she failed. "Ok, Ivy. Spill it." It was not a request, but a polite demand. Ivy lowered her gaze to the cup in her hand but remained silent. "Phantom?" that one single word from Striker was all it took.

"Oh, Justice, Phantom's one of the most amazing men! There's been no one since Keith and..." One lone tear slipped down Ivy's cheek. She steeled herself and explained what had happened in the kitchen. Well, not the kiss, but the part where she asked about his past. "I blew it, Justice! I ruined any chance I might have had!"

Justice leaned forward in his chair and covered her small hand with his large one. She looked at him, grateful for the comforting gesture. "Now you listen to me. I know my boy and he's got it bad for you. Maybe you don't see it like I do, but it's not easy for him. Just like you and Keith, he's got a story, too." He hesitated a bit and sighed. "It's not a story I'd normally tell but I think you need to hear it. I think you need to understand." Justice cleared his throat and continued with a pained expression on his face. "Phantom was married before." Ivy's eyes grew large. This wasn't exactly what she'd expected to hear. "It was the only woman Phantom had ever loved. They were perfect for each other. They understood the other's professions because she was special ops, too. They worked together as much as they could manage, always had each other's backs, and the rest of ours, too." Justice stared at the floor, eyes not seeing what he was looking at, but seeing the past. "One time, they got assigned to different missions a world apart. She was assigned to be in Japan, he in Brazil. Her team had worked reconnaissance for about sixty days before they went in to bust some big-time drug dealers. Unfortunately, the shipment that they were supposed to get that day was a set up from a different drug kingpin. It was to take the same dealers out that she was planning to. The plan got mighty fucked up and she was caught in the crosshairs. We were told she died instantly. Bullets to the heart, brain and spinal column. We lost three good people that day. That was four years ago. Phantom has never forgiven himself. He didn't want her to go on that mission and said as much but she pushed and he caved. Still hard for him to talk about."

Silent tears rolled down Ivy's face as she listened to his story. "I had no idea. It's never quite what you expect, is it?"

"Fraid not." Justice looked into Ivy's eyes. "You didn't mess things up, Ivy. Trust me. Why don't you go up and see him? Let him know it's ok. Oh...and one more thing. I haven't seen him look at anyone since then the way he looks at you."

Ivy didn't even have to think about it. She nodded, stood and walked to the doorway. She stopped abruptly and walked back to Justice, wrapping her arms around him. "Thank you." Simple and heartfelt.

Ivy climbed the stairs and walked softly to the last door. Phantom was behind this door. That realization made her suddenly hesitant. What if he didn't want her? She pushed the thought from her head and forced herself to lightly knock.

Phantom's voice came immediately, low and rough. "Come."

Ivy slowly opened the door. Oh. My. God. He was lying in bed, propped up on pillows leaning against the headboard.

Sheets and a quilt were pulled up to his waist leaving his chest gloriously bare. He looked better than she'd even imagined, and she had a pretty vivid imagination that had been working overtime lately! He was looking at her when she realized she was just standing there staring. A slow grin spread on his face when he saw her taking him in, liking what she saw. She raised her eyes to meet his. He patted the spot beside him on the bed, inviting her to join him. She slowly closed the door and walked toward the bed, shyly sitting on the side of it. He looked in her eyes, noticing the tear stains on her cheeks for the first time. "Striker told you, didn't he?"

Ivy lowered her eyes. Would he be angry his friend told his story? "Yes."

The muscle in Phantom's jaw worked but it wasn't in anger. "I guess I'm glad you know. I just didn't know how to tell you."

"I'm sorry, Phantom. Truly." Her eyes were on him again, taking in the muscles she had fantasized about. What the hell? She was trying to comfort him but all she could do was drool over his smokin' hot bod! Desperate to break her slutty train of thought, she stood. "Get some sleep."

"No." Phantom's voice was nothing but a low growl. "Don't go." His warm hand was suddenly on her wrist, keeping her where she stood. His eyes told her what his words couldn't. He wanted her. In the bed with him. Now.

Ivy continued to stand there, not sure what to do. Her mind told her getting in bed with him might not be the smartest idea she'd ever had. Her body was doing its best to convince her that he would be oh so worth it. Traitorous thing! He had only loved one woman and obviously still did, so she was afraid all he would bring her was heartache. As her head and her body stood there arguing, she gasped when he did the unexpected. He stood! Completely, unabashedly nakedly stood! She couldn't help it. She looked him over thoroughly. His legs were long and toned and led up to slim hips. When she looked at his six-pack abs, she wanted to run her tongue over each and every ridge. His shoulders were broad with a chest sprinkled with a little dark hair in the middle. She followed that hairline down, down, down. He was so hard, his cock was standing vertically, its large, purplish head reaching beyond his naval. She unconsciously licked her lips and raised her eyes to his. If she hadn't been ready to go already, the look in his eyes would have had her there in an instant.

Phantom's shaded eyes looked into hers. He lowered his head and kissed her lightly. "If it isn't obvious already, let me tell you...I want you, Ivy. I want to bury myself inside you." Ivy shivered in response. He leaned down and put his arm under her knees lifting her to place her on the bed. Leaning down over her, he kissed her, letting his tongue do his talking. She gave him a little moan and raised her pelvis enough to grind against his raging hard-on. It was his turn to moan. "It doesn't seem fair for me to be the only one without clothes." His voice was raspy and close to her ear, making it hard for her to think about anything but getting him inside her. He sat up, placing a thigh on each side of hers, and pulled her into a sitting position so he could lift her sweater up over her head and toss it to the floor. He stopped to take in the sexy light pink demi bra with the little white bow situated between her cleavage. "Beautiful." He breathed as his fingers lightly ghosted over the globe of her breasts. He laid her back onto the bed and put his mouth over a nipple through the silky material. This had her gasping as he arched into him. The clasp was in the front below the bow and he undid it and slid it down her arms to her elbows. He kept his hands on her arms where he had placed the straps to keep her in place while he teased one nipple at a time with his mouth, bringing them into tight little peaks. Ivy's breath was coming out in rapid pants as he slid his mouth down her ribs until he reached the waistband of her jeans. He let go of her arms and undid the snap and zipper. He moved his body fluidly down hers until he could grasp the waistband with both hands and pull them down and off her legs and over her feet. They, too, ended up in the pile on the floor. Her panties matched her bra. A pink scrap of lace with a tiny white bow not far from the top of her sex. He put his mouth back on her, running his tongue and fingers along that little bow, catching it with his teeth and pulling it down and off her. It landed at the top of the clothing pile on the floor. He sat up and took his time looking over her naked body. It was almost more beauty than his eyes could stand and it left him speechless. He growled low in his throat as he put his mouth on her there! *Oh. Yes Please!* He let his tongue explore her folds then move up to her clit. He circled it and felt her clench involuntarily. His calloused hands were suddenly at her center where one, then two, fingers entered her. She felt breathless, dizzy, perfect! He began to pump his fingers slowly in and out then pushed them into her as far as they would go, angled them up and scissored. OH. MY. GOD! She convulsed around his fingers and tongue while he rode with her until she melted onto the bed in a sated puddle. Oh, so slowly he removed his fingers and mouth. Not being able to keep a wicked smile from his face, he stalked up her body on his hands and knees until his face was level with hers. Her eyes fluttered open and she gave him a shy smile of her own. He kissed her, letting her have a little taste of herself from his lips. He started to get up but she grabbed his arm with a questioning look. "Condom." He said in reply.

"I haven't been with anyone in years and I'm old enough not to be able to get pregnant."

Phantom's grin was huge! "Just so you know, darlin', it's been awhile for me, too, but I still get tested, and I'm clean. So, if you insist..." He left the words hang there, while his mouth came down on hers again while he guided his cock to her slick opening. The alpha male side of him wanted to take her in one smooth thrust but, since it had been awhile for her, he would take it slow. He pushed the head in and her breath caught as she wrapped her legs around his waist. He slowly started to push when her heels dug into his tight ass and she pulled him in, while she pressed up into him in one quick shove. Her move took him by surprise and he stayed seated deep within her for a moment. Fan-fucking-tastic! She started moving, urging him on, encouraging him to go harder, deeper. This was perfect! This was *right!* This woman liked it a little dirty and she felt custom made just for him! All too soon, he felt on the edge but he sure as hell wasn't going there alone. He lowered his hand to circle that little knot of nerves above her opening and within seconds, she was moaning and he came undone when he felt her walls squeezing his aching cock. With a final deep thrust, he shattered inside her. Throwing his head back, he felt like howling!

CHAPTER TWENTY-EIGHT

THE MORNING OF THANKSGIVING EVE had Murphy up and at The Joyful Café earlier than normal. She had let her customers and friends know she would be closing early today. She wanted to get to Ivy's house to help with preparations for tomorrow's big dinner. There would be six of them. Ivy, Justice, Phantom, Cassie, Riley and herself. She didn't know when the last time she had been so excited about a holiday!

She spent the morning seeing to her regulars and a few strangers getting a jump on Christmas shopping who were just stopping for a coffee break in between. Ava was working with her, bringing her own brand of good cheer. As it neared noon, Murphy turned the sign over to read closed and she and Ava started wiping down tables and getting the café ready for when they would reopen on Friday. Black Friday always brought a huge crowd, and it stayed that way from the moment they opened till the moment they closed. When Murphy was satisfied that everything was ready, she wished Ava a Happy Thanksgiving and was off to the cottage.

Murphy drove the winding Forest Road humming that same song, 'over the river and through the woods'. As she did so, she thought back to when Justice was there on the side of that very road. Boy, if someone would have told her she'd be falling for the big lug, she would have said they were crazy! But here she was, giddy with anticipation of seeing his handsome face.

She pulled into Ivy's driveway and parked the car. The cottage had always been welcoming to her, but today, with its fall wreath decorating the door and electric candles burning in the windows, it was irresistible! Of course, it couldn't have anything to do with the hot man waiting inside!

She grabbed her purse along with the bag of groceries she had picked up last minute and headed towards the house. The minute she stepped over the threshold, she was swept up in large, warm arms and swung around in a circle. "Stop! Stop! You're making me dizzy!" She could barely get the words out, laughing as hard as she was. Justice stopped but didn't put her feet back on the ground. Instead, he kissed the stuffing out of her. When he pulled back, she gasped. She didn't think she'd ever get tired of seeing that flash of white under those full lips with dark stubble surrounding them. He was just...beautiful.

"It took everything I had in me to not come meet you at your car, but we don't want Tucker seeing us so I had to wait *hours* for you to walk that pretty ass in the house! His gaze was downright wicked and she was glad Ivy and Phantom weren't right there with them. Her smile grew even larger.

He finally lowered her to the floor and released her, taking the bag from her arms, he led the way into the kitchen where Ivy was washing a few cups at the sink.

"Hello, Dear. Everything go ok at the café today? Ivy dried her hands on a kitchen towel and walked over to Murphy to give her a tight squeeze.

"It went great! Everyone has the holiday spirit and we were busy till I closed the doors at noon." She was grateful for the café. "The trick will be surviving Black Friday." She and Ivy laughed. They both knew there was no trick to it. The busier the café was, the more Murphy thrived.

They unpacked the groceries she had brought and put them alongside the ingredients Ivy had set on the counter. Today was all about making pies and doing any prep that could be done so tomorrow they could relax and enjoy each other's company. Murphy and Ivy had been doing this same holiday ritual for as long as Murphy could remember and this year it was made even more special by having more people to enjoy it with.

Striker had walked into the surveillance room to check in with Phantom. "Murphy make it here ok?" Phantom's deep voice was protective.

"Yeah. She and Ivy are in the kitchen, looking a little like warriors ready to take on the pie battle." Striker's grin was wide.

"Good. Cuz' I was getting' tired of you pacing around the house." It felt good to Phantom to be able to tease Striker. "Course now I'll have to put up with that shit-eating grin of yours for the rest of the day. Don't know which is worse." Striker rolled his eyes but they both laughed as Phantom clicked the alarm over that would let them know if Tucker made a move, and they both made their way into the kitchen.

"Ladies." Phantom tipped an imaginary hat as he walked through the kitchen doorway.

"Well, hello, Phantom!" Murphy came around to give him a quick kiss on the cheek. "Happy Thanksgiving Eve!" Phantom chuckled and turned his gaze on Striker. Striker glared back. Phantom winked at him, making Striker's eyebrows pull down and his jaw tighten. Phantom reached out an arm patting his friend on the back.

"Easy, big guy. No one's trying to steal your girl."

Murphy turned at this to look at Striker. She couldn't help but blush a little as her smile grew. Geez! Who knew his Neanderthal caveman tendencies would do it for her! But just looking at the glare he had given Phantom had her girly parts tingling. Ok...back to the pies.

Phantom was still chuckling as he walked over to where Ivy stood at the counter. She was scooping flour into a large bowl. "How can I help, Darlin'?" His voice was low and smooth and he leaned in and kissed the side of her neck.

Murphy had looked in their direction when she heard Phantom's question. Her eyes grew to saucer size when she saw him place a light kiss on the side of Ivy's neck. Her head swung around quickly as her gaze landed on Striker's. Her eyebrows gave him a what the hell look as she nodded her head in their direction. Striker grinned that grin again and shrugged his shoulders. "I think there's something in the water." His voice was a stage whisper so Phantom and Ivy would know they were being talked about.

Ivy turner her attention toward Murphy who noticed Ivy had a hint of a blush across her cheeks. She didn't say anything but gave Murphy a quick wink with a shoulder shrug of her own and turned back to her flour, and her man. Her man. She sighed. At least for now.

All four of them busied themselves in the kitchen. Ivy was mixing dough, Murphy was putting together the pie filling and they had assigned some vegetable chopping to the men. Laughter filled the little kitchen as they all went about their tasks. Murphy and Ivy exchanged looks that said this was the way a holiday should be. Phantom and Striker felt it, too. Ivy put music on and began to dance in that same way Phantom had first seen her do.

"Not without me, you don't." He laughed as he stepped in beside her and started moving. Murphy and Striker stared open-mouthed for a minute before they both broke out in big guffaws and joined in the dancing! Arms and legs flailed, asses shook, shoulders shimmied and laughter rang out. *Now, this was how it was done!*

CHAPTER TWENTY-NINE

THANKSGIVING DAY came and it was perfect! Phantom had foregone the guest bedroom for Ivy's and if he had his way, this would be how it would stay. Murphy had been a little shy about spending the night there with Striker, but Ivy had assured her it was ok, so she and Striker had shared the guest bedroom. There was no activity next door except the occasional glimpse of Tucker in his living room or kitchen.

Ivy put the turkey in the oven then the four of them had their coffee at the kitchen table surrounded by pies left out overnight to cool. Any awkwardness between Ivy and Murphy for sleeping with their men under Ivy's roof had vanished and the four of them being there together felt natural and right.

Cassie and Riley would be joining the foursome at noon so Ivy excused herself to go shower and get ready to greet more guests. Phantom thought about going with her but decided against it. He knew that number one – if he got in the shower with her, they'd never be ready in time, and number two – Ivy needed a little time to process what was happening so fast between them.

One by one, they abandoned the kitchen table, wandering off to get themselves ready for the day. Murphy turned the television on to the Macy's Thanksgiving Parade since that was another tradition she shared with Ivy. The announcer's voices rang out as the house bustled with showers running, hair dryers working overtime and closet and bedroom doors opening and closing. Within an hour, Ivy and Murphy were back in the kitchen with the promise that Phantom and Striker would be there as soon as they checked on the equipment.

Murphy stood close to Ivy and, giving her a little push with her hip, said "He really likes you, Aunt Ivy. He's can't take his eyes off you!"

"Really? I mean...yes...uh...I like him a little, too, Dear." Ivy's blush was faint but not unnoticed by Murphy and she gave a little snort.

"Auntie, a little? Puh-lease! You wouldn't be able to fool anyone with those cow eyes batting his way every two seconds!" This had Ivy and Murphy laughing out loud. The more they laughed, the funnier it got and, by the time the men walked into the room, the women were holding their sides with tears of laughter sliding down their cheeks. Phantom and Striker exchanged confused looks, shrugged and walked out to sit in front of the parade on tv. This got the ladies howling all over again, laughing until their sides hurt.

Cassie and Riley showed up a few minutes before noon with food in hand. Cassie had made her famous – her words – cherry delight dessert and a side dish made with some sort of rice and mushrooms. It smelled delicious! "Yoo hoo" Cassie yelled as she walked in the door. She stopped at the sound and turned to raise an eyebrow at Riley who was holding the door open for her. He grinned and nodded his head towards the noise. They entered the kitchen to find all four of their friends cleaning what looked like a pie off the floor or, at the very least, trying to. They were laughing so hard, it was difficult to tell. But that wasn't all. Said pie looked like it had been smeared over the faces of everyone in the room and they were all laughing hysterically. Riley motioned for Cassie to check out Striker's behind where it looked like the pie had been originally stuck. Pumpkin was literally dripping off the back of his jeans!

The laughter died down a bit when Phantom noticed Cassie and Riley standing in the doorway, grinning. They all just stopped and stared for a minute, that is, until Phantom picked up what was left of the pie from the floor and hurled it at the doorway hitting Riley right in the forehead. Bullseye! The laughter was almost deafening at that point with Cassie joining in. Riley tried to look pissed but he couldn't manage it. Pretty soon, he was laughing, too.

Phantom then sauntered over to give him a man hug making sure he smeared the pumpkin just a little. "Happy Thanksgiving, Wildman! You're looking well, or at least you were until you came in here." Everyone broke out in laughter again, and through her grin, Cassie gave Riley a what the hell look as she mouthed 'Wildman?'

After about another hour, everyone was cleaned up, along with the kitchen and the women busied themselves tending to last minute meal preparations. The men, after being assured the women didn't need them underfoot, retired to the surveillance room where Phantom and Striker filled Riley in on the plan to take down Tucker. Riley listened intently and nodded once. "Let me know when and where and I'll be there if you need me."

"Thanks, brother. We knew we could count on you. If things go according to plan, we shouldn't need your assistance. But if this shit goes sideways, we'll let you know, as always." Striker said as he clapped his friend on the back, hard enough to take a lesser man down. Ah...friendship.

The ladies called for the men to join them in the kitchen where Ivy had pulled up a small table next to the one at the banquette. As the men entered, she handed them dishes to be placed there so they could pass food at the table instead of buffet style from the counter. The men made quick work out of moving the food bowls and they all seated themselves around the banquette. Ivy cleared her throat and reached her hands out indicating for everyone else to do the same. As they all clasped hands and bowed their heads, Ivy gave thanks for her new friends and her family and sent up a prayer that the men would remain safe in their endeavor.

The food was passed around and everyone talked at once. Striker paused and looked around, taking in every bit of it he could. This is how it's supposed to be. His eyes lit on Murphy who talked animatedly to Riley sitting next to her, something about the café business. She was smiling wide and gesturing with her hands and Striker was dumbstruck. *I love you.* What the hell? It's definitely too early for *that.* Fingers snapped in front of his face and he turned to see Phantom grinning that knowing grin of his. He winked at Striker and received a frown for his efforts. Then Phantom continued to talk to the group as though he hadn't caught Striker lost in thoughts of forever.

When dinner was over and pie was served, it started the laughter all over again. Most said they'd had enough pie for a lifetime, thank you very much, and opted for Cassie's Cherry Delight. The fun continued through clean up when everyone retired to the living room to put their feet up. With lights low, the conversation interesting, and appetites satisfied, the evening passed in blissful joy. Best. Thanksgiving. Ever!

CHAPTER THIRTY

MURPHY LEFT IVY'S on Thanksgiving night to return to her own house. As she had to get up earlier than usual, she convinced Justice to stay behind. She had to get *some* rest before facing the crowds on Black Friday, right?

Humming in the car on her way home, she drove slowly enough to admire recently put up Christmas lights throughout her neighborhood. She entered her house where she promptly took a hot shower and got ready for bed. She made herself a cup of herbal tea and carried it in on a small tray. Happiness surrounded her as she pulled the quilt up under her arms and grabbed the book off her nightstand. She was just a little wound up to fall asleep so she read a few chapters while she enjoyed her tea. Regretting leaving Justice at Ivy's house, she turned off the light, convinced herself that she did the right thing and finally fell into a deep sleep.

Murphy woke with a start when her alarm rang the next morning. She had to concentrate to remember what day it was. Oh! Black Friday! She threw the covers back and made her way into the kitchen for her first cup of coffee. She put a special flavor in her Keurig and waited the short time for it to brew. After adding some sugar and creamer, she took it with her into the bathroom to begin getting ready for work. Knowing she wanted to be early today, she had been mindful enough to lay out a pair of jeans and a dark blue sweater the night before. She quickly showered and pulled on her clothes. After putting on some mascara and a little lip gloss, she pulled her hair up in a messy ponytail, grabbed her bag and left for The Joyful Café. She was looking forward to today. Black Friday was always filled with old friends and new friends taking a break from all the crazy shopping and she loved seeing them all. Not to mention, all the money she'd rake in!

She arrived at the café earlier than usual and so did Jeff, the baker. He knew Murphy's schedule well enough to know she would be extra early this morning so he wanted to make sure she had everything she needed early, too. Murphy's eyes widened when she saw Jeff then narrowed just a bit in a teasing fashion. "So, you knew I was early today, Jeff?" Murphy said with a teasing grin.

"Yep." Jeff was eyeing her knowing she had some smartass comment she was just dying to get out.

"Stalking me?" she asked, raising a perfectly groomed eyebrow.

"Yep." Jeff chuckled.

She laughed and went about the business of selecting not only what she usually bought, but some extra goodies from him, too. She knew her customers well enough to know they would not only need coffee, but pastries and homemade breads, too.

"I honestly don't know how you do it, Jeff. You must stay up all night to get everything ready. And it all looks so delicious!" Murphy sniffed appreciatively at all the wondrous baked goods in Jeff's delivery van. "I would weigh a thousand pounds if I did what you do!"

Jeff smiled, appreciating her comments. "I'm like a baby. My days and nights are completely messed up! I work all night and sleep during the day. As for eating it all? Although I still taste test, I don't really eat a lot of it when I'm baking. You wouldn't either if you did it all the time...which I'm glad you don't, by the way." He gave Murphy a quick wink. "Well, I'm off before the savages arrive! Enjoy Black Friday!" Murphy gave a little wave as she watched his van pull away from the back of her café.

Ava arrived just seconds after Jeff's van rounded the corner. She exited her car, threw her big purse over her shoulder and walked up to the door Murphy was holding open for her. "Good morning, Murphy!" As usual, Ava had a bright smile on her face. "Ready for crazy Black Friday?"

"As ready as I'll ever be! Wait till you see the special pastries and breads I got from Jeff today. That man is a wizard with an oven!" They walked into the kitchen through the back room and began to put all the delicious delicacies out on the counter. Ava was practically drooling! They chose the prettiest pastries to be put on platters in the display case, keeping out a few to cut up and leave on top of the case on a sample plate. Full loaves of bread were put in baskets on counter tops and some were left out to be sliced for toast or small sandwiches for those who wanted something a little more substantial to eat.

Murphy and Ava looked everything over twice before deciding it was perfect and the doors could be opened. And so it begins.

Murphy switched the sign on the door from closed to open, unlocked the door and held it open for her first customers. Four women walked in giggling and all talking at once. Murphy told them to sit anywhere and she would be right over to take their orders. They took a seat by the windows and put down packages they had already purchased even though it was only five o'clock in the morning! Murphy walked to the table with pen and tablet in hand. "Good morning, ladies! Good shopping already?" she asked as she approached the table. The ladies all seemed to talk at once, all excited about their purchases. The bell over the door jingled and all four heads turned towards it. The table grew quiet and Murphy followed their gaze towards the door. Oh.

Yeah. She got it. The ladies had become tongue tied over a tall dark, handsome man walking in. *Her* tall, dark, handsome man. Justice's eyes immediately landed on Murphy and his white teeth appeared bright against his dark skin when he broke into that panty-melting grin.

"Wow!" One of the ladies found her voice at the table. "I'd like *him* in my stocking this Christmas!"

Another one joined in. "Yeah. Tell me where they sell him on Black Friday and I'll be there with my checkbook, credit cards and the deed to my house!" She fanned herself with her hand and they all giggled.

"Sorry, ladies." Murphy broke in wearing a grin. "I'm afraid that one is taken. But I'll pass along with compliments." She winked at the ladies and continued. "Now, what can I get for you this morning?" Looking appropriately embarrassed, they each gave Murphy their orders and silently agreed to leave extra big tips.

Murphy slid back behind the counter and started plating the lady's orders and pouring coffee. Ava had gotten Justice's favorite coffee for him and he had taken a place at the counter so he could chat with Murphy as she worked. "Did you get a good night's sleep?" he asked. His voice was deep and sexy, and Murphy was afraid it would melt the icing on the pastries.

"I had a bit of trouble getting to sleep because..." she walked closer to where he was sitting, putting a little extra wiggle in her walk, "I was regretting asking you to stay at Aunt Ivy's." Murphy lowered her lashes and looked at Justice from underneath them. She could feel the heat of him across the counter. Whew! This man was going to be the death of her! "While I'm thinking of it, you have a fan club sitting at the table by the windows." She tilted her head in that direction. Justice grinned but never bothered to even look. "I only have eyes for you, Wells." He reached across the counter, cupping his hand behind her head and pulling her close, he kissed her lightly on the lips. *Yep. Death of me.*

The bell tinkled over the door in quick succession and Murphy was kept busy for a while, getting orders and making specialty coffees. After walking one of her favorite customers to the door, she turned and hurried over to Justice. "He's here!" she whispered breathlessly. Justice gave her a questioning look. "That man living next to Ivy. He's coming in right now!" she grabbed Justice's hand, leading him into the backroom, where he could keep an eye on the front without being seen. "I'm assuming you don't want him to see you, right?" Murphy said as the door closed behind them. "You can see the front through this window without them seeing you. I'll come get you when he leaves." Justice thanked her and she quickly went back to the front to help Ava.

"That creepy guy is back." Ava whispered to Murphy coming up beside her.

"I know. I told Justice how seriously creeped out we were last time, so he's gonna watch him from the back."

The man had come in but hadn't made a move to sit down. He just hovered by the door for a while keeping his eyes glued to Murphy. She tried to shake it off and walked towards him. "Good morning!" she said, trying to sound as normal as possible. "You can take a seat wherever you can find one."

Tucker made some sort of hissing sound in his throat which made Murphy jump a little, but she quickly recovered and plastered a smile back on her face. Joseph Tucker's beady eyes never left her and he seemed to be having difficulty speaking, but finally he croaked out "Coffee. Black. To go." The man didn't even try to smile at her.

Murphy hurried behind the counter and got his to-go order. He held out money with a dirty hand and she took it and returned some change. "Thank you." She muttered. He turned and walked to the door but stopped before he opened it and turned again, scanned the café, and returned his beady eyes to Murphy. After staring blankly at her for several seconds, he turned and walked through the door.

Murphy quickly hurried to the back room as Justice came through the door. She was breathing hard as she looked at him. "What the hell was that?" she asked but didn't really expect an answer. Justice looked positively fierce. "Don't let him back in without me or Phantom being here. Call us right away if that sonofabitch shows up. Promise me, Wells." Murphy nodded, feeling better that she and Ava wouldn't have to be alone with him. There was just something off about the man.

Justice said his goodbyes with promises to see her later and returned to his truck. He wanted to get back to Ivy's place to see if Tucker had headed home and to let Phantom know what had happened. He had a sinking suspicion Tucker was starting to put pieces of the puzzle together and those pieces included the person he'd come to think of as his, Murphy Wells.

CHAPTER THIRTY-ONE

HE'D WOKEN this Black Friday morning like he was going to jump out of his skin so he thought he would go for a ride but ended up at the café. He'd known he should have made conversation. Known he should have a least tried to smile. But when he stood before her, the fires of hate licked all around him and he could barely manage not reaching out to rap his hands around her delicate throat and squeeze. He hadn't seen the light go out in anyone's eyes for a while now and wanted to see it go out in hers.

Doom clouded his senses. *That bitch!* He thought, having no idea of what he should do about it. The only thing he knew for sure was she visited the cottage next door regularly and once she had brought *him*! His mind drifted back to that day. His memories brought forth the rumble of the motorcycle, the blond woman taking off her helmet to look up adoringly at a large man. That man taking off his helmet and turning...his...head...POW! That was when he'd recognized the bastard for one of them that had been on his trail. He'd thought he'd lost them, thought he could maybe start to live free.

Without even being aware, he had walked to his car from the café and driven it to the driveway of his grandfather's house. He pulled the car into the garage, closed the garage door as quietly as he could, and went into the house, unaware of the man next door watching and hearing his every more.

Phantom waited until Tucker was seemingly situated in his usual chair by the window before getting up to refresh his own coffee in Ivy's kitchen. He didn't see when Tucker dropped a cigarette from a freshly opened pack onto the floor and watched as it rolled beneath the window. Reaching for the cigarette, he ducked his head under the windowsill, stretching himself until his fingers found it. Holding onto it like a lifeline, he raised his head back up but didn't clear the sill and *thump!* Hit the back of his head on the windowsill's edge. Angry with himself, but wanting to take it out on something, he glared at the sill until, *what's this?* His eyes landed on a small contraption mounted under the sill with precision. The average person would not have recognized it for what it was, but he was not the average person, now was he. He sat up quickly, hoping whoever was watching him wouldn't have noticed that he had discovered their little secret. He sat like a stone, cigarette forgotten, thoughts whirring in his head like bees in a jar. *What now?*

CHAPTER THIRTY-TWO

STRIKER MADE it back to Ivy's cottage in record time, using his usual path to her garage. He was out of the truck and into the house within seconds. "Phantom!" he called entering the house. Phantom was suddenly in front of him, startling him, being that he was a little jumpy after witnessing that creepy little bastard eyeing his woman. "Jesus! I hate when you do that!" he breathed out, giving his friend his best glare.

"I came by my name naturally, remember?" Phantom said, calmly as ever.

'Yeah. I'm just not used to you using that stealth shit on me is all!"

"What's got you acting like your pants are full of fire ants this morning? I thought you went to get your fill of your woman. You should be all unicorns and butterflies!" His mouth twisted up into a self-satisfied grin. Phantom always enjoyed getting under Striker's skin as brothers tend to do.

Striker ignored the barb. "That sonofabitch from next door paid a little visit to my woman at the café today!" Anger rolled through Phantom as a muscle in his jaw twitched. "Murphy seated me in the back so I could watch. He had come in once before and she let me know how creeped out she and Ava had been. This bastard even creeped *me* out."

Phantom knew Tucker had left, of course, and also knew he had returned home and settled himself in his usual chair. The alarm was set so they would know if he left the house. Striker's eyes pierced Phantom. "I'm not letting this go on much longer, man. If something doesn't go down soon, we're gonna have to make it go down."

AS TUCKER SAT as still as a statue, his mind was telling him if there was one camera and microphone, there were more. The first thing he'd have to do would be sweep the house for bugs. Electronic bugs. No time like the present. Having used these types of electronics himself, he knew just what to look for. The kitchen would be first. Knowing they could be watching, he strode into the kitchen like he did every day and opened the refrigerator door, pretending to peruse the contents. While his head was bent towards the insides of the fridge, his eyes were roaming around the edges of the kitchen. He locked on it after a couple minutes, seeing it in the corner of the ceiling above the kitchen cabinets. Hmmmm. That's exactly where he would have placed it, too. Good coverage. And most people never would have seen it. He was not most people. He shut the refrigerator door and moved on. Changing out bathroom towels allowed him to sweep the bathroom without drawing undue attention. Finding no bugs there or in the hallway left only the bedroom to look over. Since changing the towels worked so well, he decided to change out the sheets, not that he slept all that often. But this would throw off his onlookers if need be. He gave the bedroom a thorough once over coming up with nothing there, either. Now if it were him keeping surveillance on someone, he would make sure he knew of their comings and goings, so the front and back doors would be alarmed. He wouldn't even bother to look, knowing they were. He'd let the bastards know only what he wanted them to know from now on.

CHAPTER THIRTY-THREE

THE CAFÉ HAD kept Murphy and Ava busy all morning, not giving them any chance to dwell on the weird visit from the evil little man earlier. It was all but forgotten when Cassie came in like the hurricane she was. Murphy looked her over. Her red hair was falling in loose curls around her shoulders. Her coat was short, fitted and the most wonderful Christmas green color Murphy had ever seen. Black leggings hugged her voluptuous curves and it was all topped off by camel colored over-the-knee boots with dangerously high heels. Yep. Hurricane.

"Hey, Murph!" Cassie called as she glided in through the door. "Thought you might be ready for a little break." She looked at her best friend expecting to see someone who had been on their feet all morning serving a bunch of grumpy assed shoppers out trying to save a buck before Christmas. But what she saw instead made her smile. There was her friend looking like someone who had *enjoyed* being on their feet all morning serving a bunch of grumpy assed shoppers out trying to save a buck before Christmas. Cassie laughed with the irony of she, herself, being one of the shoppers saving a buck before Christmas!

"Hey, yourself! Looks like you hit the jackpot." Murphy eyed the bags in Cassie's hands. "Anything in there for me?" she fluttered her eyelashes pretending to be so innocent.

Cassie laughed. "You'll just have to wait and see. Got time to sit and have a cup?" She had already placed herself at a table that had just opened by the window. Murphy turned to get their cups but Ava waved her away saying she'd bring them over.

"So, where's your handsome shadow this morning?" Murphy laughed as she asked.

"I think he might be paying a visit to Justice and Phantom, or he might be on the phone working some shit out with the band, or, and I think this is the best bet, he might be giving himself a little break and napping on the couch!" They both laughed at that. "I wanted to come out by myself today. You know how much I love shopping and Black Friday is the best! Plus, I wanted to stop and take a look at you, make sure you're ok."

Murphy rolled her eyes at her friend. "I'm good, Cass. You know you'd be the first to know if I wasn't."

"So, Phantom and Ivy, huh? Didn't see that coming!" Cassie's eyes were wide and round. "But after spending the day with them yesterday, it was hard to miss!"

Murphy nodded her head in agreement. "Yeah. At first, I was a bit shocked, but now? It's kind of sweet. She deserves a man like Phantom. Tall. Handsome. Protective. Pure alpha male, that one. I haven't seen her this happy since...well...hmmm, I've never seen her like this! And I worry about her sometimes, being out there on Forest Road all by herself. Although I did find out she keeps a sawed-off shotgun and knows how to use it!"

Cassie actually laughed. "Somehow, that doesn't surprise me in the least. I can see Ivy has a bit of Annie Oakley in her. That woman is an inspiration to us all!" They continued talking about the upcoming holiday until Murphy had to excuse herself to get back to work. A second crowd was starting to gather and it wouldn't be like Murphy at all to leave Ava to do all the work. They hugged their goodbyes and the hurricane known as Cassie swept out the door.

CHAPTER THIRTY-FOUR

JOSEPH TUCKER waited till it was good and dark. He had stewed all day and what he came up with was it all boiled down to that fucking bitch living in the yellow cottage. He couldn't possibly imagine being so careless that the large man followed *his* trail here. He would never be careless enough to leave a trail! He wasn't like other so called 'normal' people, remember? So, the fluke of this fucked up situation was that somehow, the big man knew *her*. So, if it wasn't for *her*, he wouldn't be caught up in this shit storm. If he could take care of her, then lay low for a while, there would be no reason for them to come back to him. He was feeling just crazy enough for the plan to make sense.

Knowing without looking that there were alarms on both doors, he opened the bedroom window and crept out. He stopped just outside and checked his Glock G19. It felt good to have his gun in his hands again. Palming it, he crept around the side of the house, keeping in the shadows of the dark night. Stopping at the house's corner, he stood and watched the cottage for several moments. Everything seemed normal. Same lights were on that were always on, no shadows crossing over windows. It looked like it always did.

Keeping his small frame as low to the ground as possible, he ran across the lot separating the houses, not stopping until he was under the large picture window framing the kitchen in the back of the cottage. He stayed down below the window, waiting to catch his breath. His hand felt sweaty against the handle of the gun. He moved it from his right hand to his left and wiped his sweaty palm down the leg of his dirty jeans. Having dried it enough, he once again held the gun in position in his dominant right hand.

Once his breathing had evened out, he slowly lifted his head in the corner of the window watching for any movement in the kitchen. And then he saw her. She was doing something at the counter. He couldn't see what it was exactly but it looked like she was mixing something in a large bowl. It would be easy to just aim and pull the trigger right now. Just put the gun to the window. Just point it at her and watch her fall to the floor. He felt himself smile, baring his ugly yellowed teeth. It would be so easy. But no. He wanted to see her. He wanted to look into her eyes so he could see her fear. He wanted to taste it. To hear it. To smell it.

Phantom had taken Striker's truck into town to pick up a few things Ivy needed from the store. He had volunteered for grocery duty thinking Ivy could use a little time alone. Striker had set the switch so the alarm would sound if Tucker left his house, then he laid back on the cot in the surveillance room. He hadn't been sleeping well and was just going to close his eyes for a little while. He could hear Ivy moving around in the kitchen. He could hear her radio playing softly.

Ivy was stirring cake batter when she heard a soft knock on the kitchen door. She wondered why Phantom would be coming in that way. She set the bowl on the counter and grabbed the dishtowel, wiping her hands as she reached for the door knob. She turned the knob and was prepared to greet Phantom. Her intake of breath was sharp when she saw the man from next door standing in the doorway pointing a gun straight at her heart.

A grisly leer showed his yellowed teeth as his voice came out as a croak. "You fucking bitch! You're the reason for all of thisss!" Then he pulled the trigger.

CHAPTER THIRTY-FIVE

IVY WAS IN slow motion. She knew Joseph Tucker had spoken. She'd never forget the tone of his voice, his ugly yellowed teeth and the spit that had exited his mouth as he spoke. Then she had felt a strong hand grasp her arm and pull just as pain ripped through her shoulder. The force of the pain had spun her. She barely remembered a very loud noise then blackness. Nothingness.

Striker had just closed his eyes when he thought he heard Ivy move towards the back door. He strained to hear. Yep. The door knob was being turned. He was on his feet and in the kitchen before it registered who was standing outside the door. The gun that he kept tucked in the back of his jeans waistband was in his hand instantly. He didn't think. He just reacted. His hand grabbed Ivy and pulled her aside while he came around her other side, aimed and fired.

He saw Tuckers eyes go wide for a split second, trying to register what was happening. The bullet fired from Striker's weapon found its target and took Tucker out with one shot. Striker watched as his bullet lodged itself between Tucker's beady eyes. For a moment there was nothing. No blood. No reaction. Then the back of Tucker's head no longer existed as he became nothing but a crumpled mass on the grass outside the steps of Ivy's kitchen.

Striker had his phone to his ear before he could even lower himself to Ivy. 911. Ambulance on the way.

He hadn't noticed Phantom come in until he heard the bag of groceries drop to the floor and felt his friend at his side. Phantom had assessed the situation quickly and efficiently like they had been taught and immediately knew what had happened. He saw the blood seeping from Ivy's body and tore open her blouse so he could locate the source. The bullet had entered at her left shoulder but had not exited. He grabbed the kitchen towel lying beside her on the floor and put pressure on it over the entrance wound. He and Striker worked as a team until the wails of the ambulance could be heard. As the sirens grew closer, Striker went through the house to the front door to direct them in.

The ambulance crew fastened an oxygen mask on Ivy and laid her on a stretcher. Phantom's heart was in his throat as he noticed she had never moved. Striker and Phantom loaded themselves in the truck as the ambulance pulled away. Phantom drove as Striker worked quickly from his phone. Arrangements were made with the Feds to collect Tucker's body and Murphy was instructed to meet them at the hospital.

CHAPTER THIRTY-SIX

STRIKER AND PHANTOM made quite the picture as they burst through the Emergency Room doors. They stopped at the reception desk and questioned the nurse on the whereabouts of Ivy. As the nurse was starting to explain the HIIPA rules and how they were not family, Murphy entered the ER. Coming up to stand between the two men, she announced to the nurse that she was family and told her she could tell these two men anything she would tell her. They were then informed that Ivy had been taken to surgery and the doctor would be out to speak with them when she was done but it would probably be a while.

The three of them settled in the quietest corner they could find in the busy waiting room when Murphy started asking questions. "What the hell happened? Why is my aunt in surgery?" Murphy's voice was raised and Striker put his hand on her arm to try to lessen her fear.

His silver eyes locked onto hers as he spoke. "Tucker appeared at the back door." Phantom didn't have the full story either so he leaned forward putting an elbow on each thigh, listening intently. "By the time I got in the kitchen, his gun was raised. He fired a shot before I could move Ivy completely out of the way."

Phantom ran his hands through his short hair. He knew Tucker had aimed at Ivy's heart when Striker had grabbed her. He knew by where and how the bullet had entered her shoulder. Murphy didn't. She didn't know her aunt would be in the morgue right now instead of having a chance in a surgery room if it wasn't for Striker. She didn't know and from the look on her face, she didn't care.

Murphy turned on Justice, narrowing her eyes and hissing through clenched teeth. "None of this would have happened if it wasn't for you! I wouldn't be sitting in the emergency waiting room hoping that my aunt, my only living relative, will survive a fucking gunshot wound! None of this would have happened if you hadn't come into our lives! I asked you not to involve her!" Striker reached up to put his hand back on Murphy's forearm. She stood so quickly the chair tipped behind her and she shook his arm off as though it was a snake. "NO! You don't get to touch me! Don't ever touch me! You have no right! None! I want you out! Out of this ER, out of our lives! Now!" She turned and walked down the hall where she disappeared into the ladies' room.

A large hand clamped down on Striker's shoulder. Phantom. "She didn't mean it, my friend. She doesn't know. Let her cool off. She'll come around." But Striker had seen something in her eyes. Something he never wanted to see again. Blame. She blamed him, hated him. And he loved her. As they walked out into the night, he once again pulled out his phone. He told Riley that Murphy needed Cassie.

CHAPTER THIRTY-SEVEN

MURPHY CLOSED THE DOOR to the ladies' room and burst into tears. She leaned back against the door, shoulders shaking with grief. *How could this have happened? What will I do without him? What will I do with her?* She walked to the sink and looked in the mirror. She didn't even recognize herself. Her face was red, her eyes were swollen and her hair was a mess. But it was more than that. It was the look in her eyes. She had been downright cruel to Justice. She had watched the light go out of those handsome silver eyes as she had spoken to him so harshly. Standing there staring into the mirror, she did recognize one thing...she recognized that her heart was breaking. Taking a deep breath, she squared her shoulders, splashed some water on her face and with head held high, walked out of the ladies' room. It was easier to hold on to the anger. And she needed to focus on the most important thing right now and that was Ivy.

Murphy reentered the waiting room, glancing at where the three of them had been sitting. They were gone. He was gone. That was good, wasn't it? That's what she had asked for. Taking a seat in the opposite corner, she looked up as the ER doors slid open and was surprised to see Cassie.

Cassie's eyes scanned the room. When she found Murphy, she hurried over and threw her arms around her best friend. "Oh my God, Murph! Have you heard anything? Has the doctor come out yet?"

Murphy hugged her friend back. "How did you know I was...oh...Justice." It became more of a statement than a question as it dawned on Murphy.

Cassie took in Murphy's somewhat tattered appearance, knowing she had been crying. "You ok? Justice didn't say much to Riley but it was clear from what he didn't say that something happened between the two of you. The most he said was that you needed me."

"He just can't help meddling but his time I guess I'm glad he did. I'm glad you're here."

"Soooo...you want to talk about it?" Cassie asked. Murphy searched her friend's face. They had shared practically everything since the day they met. But she wasn't sure she could go there right now. "No. Let's just wait for the doctor. The first thing is to make sure Ivy is going to be ok."

Cassie agreed, knowing that Murphy needed the anger she was feeling toward Justice right now. They could talk about it later. She reached out and squeezed Murphy's hand then they both sat back into the uncomfortable chairs and waited.

CHAPTER THIRTY-EIGHT

STRIKER AND PHANTOM made their way back to Ivy's cottage. The Feds were just cleaning up the last of the mess that had been Joseph Tucker. They had loaded a body bag in their van and were cleaning up the surrounding area. They were known for never leaving any evidence at a crime scene.

Phantom bent down to pick up the bag of groceries he had dropped when he had walked in last time. A carton of eggs had broken and he ran a dishcloth under the faucet and started wiping the floor.

Striker lowered himself onto the bench at the banquette and put his head in his hands. They hadn't spoken during the ride from the hospital. Phantom knew he needed time to process.

Phantom finished cleaning up the floor. Looking over to where Ivy had lain on the floor, he noticed the Feds had already cleaned up her blood.

Striker stood and silently went into the surveillance room. He started unplugging equipment and wrapping wires.

Phantom left him to do it while he went next door. He once again picked the lock on the back door and went in to remove their equipment. He left the house exactly as it had been before their equipment had been put in place.

He hauled the equipment bag back inside the cottage and into the surveillance room where he noticed Striker had started taking bags to the truck. He turned to see his friend coming through the garage entrance.

"Hey, man." Phantom said. "How bout I take it from here? You can go upstairs and pack up whatever you have there." Striker nodded once and headed for the stairs. He paused in the doorway outside the room he had shared with Murphy. He closed his eyes and rubbed his hands through his dark hair. *Murphy.* Forcing his legs to move, he went about the business of packing the small amount of things he had brought. Without looking back, he walked down the stairs and out to the truck.

Phantom was putting a bag in the truck and looked up when he heard Striker. "Last one, brother. Anything else you need to get?"

"No." That one word spoke volumes.

They piled themselves into the truck and went back down the path and out on to the road.

CHAPTER THIRTY-NINE

MURPHY AND CASSIE were sitting in silence in the ER waiting room when the automatic double doors opened down the hall. The doctor walked the hallway with her eyes on the floor. As she entered the waiting room, she stopped and looked around. The crowd from earlier had thinned leaving only five people. The doctor's gaze went to Murphy and Cassie and she advanced in their direction. Murphy stood anxiously.

"Ms. Wells?" Murphy nodded. "I'm Dr. Stevens. I'm the surgeon on your aunt's case and I wanted to let you know the surgery went well. The bullet entered her left shoulder shattering her scapula. We were able to rebuild the parts we couldn't repair and she's in recovery. I don't expect her to wake up for another hour or so then she'll be groggy at best so if you'd like to go..."

"No!" The word came out a little more forcefully than Murphy had intended. She quieted herself before speaking again. "Thank you, Dr. Stevens, but I prefer to stay." She tried to smile but didn't quite pull it off.

The doctor nodded. "I understand. The prognosis is good. She will have a long road of therapy but I expect her to regain full movement. I don't know the whole story, but actually, she got lucky."

"Thank you, doctor. She's the only family I have and..." Murphy's voice broke into a sob and Cassie put an arm around her and spoke for the first time since the doctor had come out. "Thank you, doctor. We'll wait here. When do you think we could see her?"

"I'll tell the nurse to come and get you when she starts to come out of the anesthetic and they have her in a room. So, maybe a couple of hours."

Murphy and Cassie murmured more thanks and with a nod, the doctor turned and walked back down the hall and through the double doors.

CHAPTER FORTY

STRIKER DROVE to an apartment building where he and Phantom had set up rooms to use while they were in town. They'd hardly used them at all having spent most of their time at the cottage and Striker staying occasionally at Murphy's.

They pulled in front of the building's entrance but didn't bother to get out. Phantom broke the silence. "How bout I buy us a drink? Maybe some dinner?"

"A drink sounds good." Striker pulled away from the building. "Where to?" Phantom named a little place he knew they could eat and get drunk if needed without any trouble.

After being seated, they ordered beers and burgers. The waitress was flirty and efficient, bringing their beers immediately. "Ok." Phantom said. "Wanna talk about it?"

"Oh, could I? Then maybe we could braid each other's hair and play with our Barbies."

Phantom chuckled softly. "Glad to see you haven't lost your sense of humor, you sarcastic ass. And, since you don't want to talk, I've got something I want to talk to you about." Striker raised his eyebrows and Phantom continued. "I guess I've been feeling kinda restless lately and tired of the kind of life we've been living. I talked about it to Ivy and I'd like to settle down. I'd like to do it here." His gaze held his friend's. Striker was important to him and he wanted his opinion. Maybe his blessing.

The one side of Striker's mouth turned up. "Man, you and I have always been in sync, but this shit's gettin' scary. I'm feeling the same way about getting out of the biz and settling down. Here. I've been thinking about it for a while and now that I know where your head's at, I have a proposition for you." The waitress brought their burgers along with a couple more beers. "I want to open a little pub. Nothing fancy, just a place where you can get a drink, maybe listen to a band, shoot some pool, ya know, like a neighborhood bar. Someplace ladies can come to and feel safe. Someplace men can belly up to the bar after work. Someplace that's mine... annnnd....yours? I'm thinkin' I would like a partner, brother, and you would be the one I would choose. What do ya think?"

Phantom was smiling. "Do you have the place picked out yet?"

"I haven't gone to see it yet. But there's some property with a building on it down on Pine Street. It looks like it needs work but it's a good location, lots of parking, and zoned commercial. I was hoping we could see it together."

"Set it up." Both smiling, Phantom held out his hand to Striker and they shook. The waitress shuddered at the good-looking picture they presented.

CHAPTER FORTY-ONE

EXACTLY TWO HOURS had passed in the waiting room of the ER when a nurse told Murphy and Cassie to follow her. They were led into a sterile hospital room where Ivy was lying in a bed, somewhat propped up on pillows. Her eyes were half open and they followed Murphy and Cassie into the room. Murphy practically ran to the bedside but hesitated to hug her aunt when she saw the tubes and bandages. "Aunt Ivy? How are you feeling?"

Ivy's throat was sore and her voice was raspy. "Been better, but I'm ok. I don't remember much after Justice grabbed me. Just pain and a loud bang. If it wasn't for Justice, though..."

"If it wasn't for Justice, we wouldn't be here! If it wasn't for Justice, you wouldn't be lying here with a gunshot wound! If it wasn't for Justice, we'd be in your kitchen right now baking for the holidays! Yeah, he's a real fucking saint!" Cassie laid her hand on Murphy's arm to stop her rant. Murphy's eyes rounded when she looked at Ivy. "I'm sorry, Auntie. But I'm going to make a rule right now. No one, and I mean NO one speaks about that man in my presence again!

Now, I'll calm down and we'll forget about him." She took a deep breath. "Can I get you anything? You need some water or ice chips?"

Ivy saw her chance. "Yes, Dear, would you be good enough to ask the nurse for a cup of ice chips? That would feel good on my throat." Murphy went out the door and padded down the hall. Ivy turned to Cassie. "What was that all about?"

Cassie shrugged her shoulders. "You know about as much as I do except I don't exactly know what happened at your house. She refuses to talk about it at all. The reason I know anything is because Justice called Riley to let him know Murphy would need me here at the hospital. I guess I'm going to have to call Justice or ask Riley to." They heard Murphy's footsteps coming down the hallway and silenced themselves.

"Here you go. Ice chips for your throat. Can you manage? I could help you."

Ivy rolled her eyes. "I had some surgery. I'm not an invalid. Although, I will admit that I'll probably be needing some help here and there for a while. Although, I'll have Phantom helping, too."

Murphy tensed but she kept her mouth shut. Not much got past Ivy though. It never had. "Murphy, I don't tell you how to live your life and just so you know, you sure as hell am not going to tell me how to live mine. If you've had an argument with that handsome man of yours, that's for you to work out. But don't be getting all tense that Phantom is going to be staying with me."

"You mean he's staying? Even though the job is done? He's not leaving like...." She left the words unsaid but Ivy and Cassie felt her unspoken pain.

Cassie's voice was soft when she spoke. "Did Justice tell you he was leaving?"

"Not in so many words. I just always knew we were never going to be a forever thing. His job takes him away. He *is* his job. *He* takes himself away. Why would that change?" Her sadness felt like a living, breathing thing. She shook her head and squared her shoulders. "Anyway, I'm happy for you, Ivy. Phantom is a good man and you deserve that!"

"Justice is a good man, too. Now, I love you both, but get out. I need some rest." Ivy smiled at her girls. They said their goodbyes and promised to check in later.

As they left the hospital, Cassie put her arm around her friend's shoulders. "Justice is a good man, Murph. You do know that, right?"

"It doesn't matter. There's no working things out. He's the cause of all this and he's leaving. Now, I meant it when I said I don't want his name mentioned anymore. I'm just going to concentrate on the café and getting Ivy back to normal."

CHAPTER FORTY-TWO

PHANTOM WANTED to see Ivy but didn't want to stir up bad feelings with Murphy so he waited till after visiting hours were over. He strode through the front door to the reception desk. He gave a crooked smile to the receptionist. "Hi, Darlin." He drawled. "I know visiting hours are over but my friend, Ivy Mays, had surgery and I wasn't able to get here till now. You'd be doing me a huge favor it you let me see her. I texted and told her I would come." The receptionist looked up, opened her mouth, then closed it again. He knew the effect he could have on women especially when he put a little more southern in his deep voice. And he knew he was using it to full effect at this moment. He raised his eyebrows at the receptionist, giving his best puppy dog look and he saw the moment she caved.

She kept her voice low. "I'm really not supposed to, but if you promise you won't stay long, you can go on up. She's in room 205."

"Thank you, Darlin." He said. She literally swooned when he threw a wink her way and sauntered down the hall to the elevators.

When he reached room 205, he knocked lightly before opening the door. A small light was on and he could see Ivy's form in the bed. He took a deep breath and was beside her in two long strides. She opened her eyes and smiled. "It's after visiting hours, Phantom. Did you flirt with some poor unsuspecting girl to get your way in here?" He just grinned down at her. "Hmmm. Too bad you don't use those powers of yours for good!" She gave a little laugh but winced with the pain it brought to her.

He felt helpless standing there. "Can I get you anything? Do you need the nurse? When was the last time you had pain medication?"

She waved the arm that hadn't been injured. "Stop mothering me. You're as bad as Murphy! I'm ok. As ok as I can be for someone who took a bullet this morning." She gave him a tired smile.

"Gonna milk that for a while, aren't you?" Phantom loved teasing her.

"You know it!" She gave a little laughed then winced again.

"I have something I want to talk to you about." Phantom hesitated until Ivy gave a go-ahead nod. "I told Striker today about my plans to quit the business and stay here. I know you and I talked about it but we never really confirmed details..."

"Stay with me." Ivy said it so suddenly, she even surprised herself!

Phantom's teeth showed white against his dark skin. "Well now, Darlin, you took all the work out of that for me, didn't ya?" His chuckle was soft and deep. "I figured you would need help getting around, and before you go all Rambo on me, I know you can take care of yourself but I'd like to help out. And besides, I'm kinda crazy about you and want to be with you." He waggled his eyebrows and she giggled. "Also, Striker asked me to partner with him. He wants to open a neighborhood pub. He's given it a lot of thought and we're looking at some property tomorrow. So, the only thing I can see that might be standing in our way is...." He hesitated, not sure she knew or how she would take it.

"Murphy." She said it before he had a chance to spit it out. He nodded once, letting her know that was exactly what was on his mind. "No need to worry. She and I had a little chat. She knows you're a good man and said I deserved one. One thing you should know, though. She has insisted none of us mention Justice's name around her. I don't know what happened between them but she doesn't know he's staying. She told Cassie and I that he was leaving town."

"I think he was saving it for a surprise, but then Tucker attacked you and she blamed Striker. I was there. I heard it all. She never even gave him a chance. I know she was upset and I told him as much. My advice was to let her cool down and hopefully, she'll come around. He still doesn't want her to know we're partnering on the pub at this time." He reached out and gave her hand a little squeeze. "I'd best be heading out. You need your rest. Has the doctor said anything about you going home?"

"She'll check on me in the morning and I'm hoping to convince her that I'd heal faster there."

Phantom considered this and agreed. "What time is she coming in?" Murphy told him seven in the morning and he said he'd be there. With a soft kiss, he left.

CHAPTER FORTY-THREE

THE NEXT DAY, Striker and Phantom stood outside the building on the property they had talked about. Striker was right. Good location. Good property. Plenty of parking. The real estate agent opened the door and led them into the building. Flicking on the light switch, he led them into what had been a bar several years back. The agent had told them the bar had been closed for several years. The owner had passed away. He had left it to his daughter but she didn't want anything to do with it. In fact, she completely ignored it until recently when she had contacted him to 'get it gone'.

The building had good bones but it had surely been neglected. There was a bar on the one side. It looked like solid mahogany but was in need of a really good cleaning. There were plenty of shelves behind the bar itself and along the wall behind it, too. Tables were crowded in the middle of the room but it didn't look like anything was really salvageable. Booths along the one wall needed to be torn out. There was a dance floor with a stage that didn't look like it was in too bad of a condition. They took a tour through a small kitchen suited for bar food if it was kept simple. And the back room had a place for a few pool tables. After carefully looking over the bathrooms and an office area in the back, they thanked the agent and told him they'd be in touch.

They drove to another bar so they could sit and discuss what they'd seen. Striker was the first to address it. "I think it's fucking perfect, man. Like I told you it needs a lot of work, but I think we could handle most of it ourselves and that would save a bundle up front. We'll contract the things we're not comfortable with like electric and plumbing. What do you think?"

"Right there with you, brother. Couldn't be much better for us. And, if the daughter doesn't want anything to do with it, I think we can get a much better price than what she's asking.

Striker's smile was wide. "So, you're in?"

"Yeah. I'm in."

CHAPTER FORTY-FOUR

PHANTOM'S TEXT pinged and he saw that Ivy was almost ready to leave the hospital. "Gotta go, brother. Ivy's ready to go home. Can't keep the lady waiting." He threw some bills on the table and Striker drove them to the apartment building where Phantom's car awaited.

Phantom showed up at the hospital just as Ivy was instructing Murphy how to pack up the rest of her things. As usual, Murphy had gone a little overboard and brought much more than Ivy would have ever needed. "Need a hand, ladies?" Phantom's deep voice boomed from the doorway of room 205. Ivy broke into a grin while Murphy ... hmmm ... looked guilty? Phantom wasn't sure what that look was but he was going to put a stop to it. Now. He walked to Ivy first and gave her a short kiss then stalked over to Murphy drawing her into a hug. Murphy went rigid as Phantom pulled her in and wrapped his big, warm arms around her back. As he held her, she softened, and put her arms around him, too. When he let her go, her eyes were shining with unshed tears. "Don't worry, Murphy. It will all work out. I know you don't want to talk about him right now." She raised a hand in protest, but he ignored it. "I won't go against your wishes. I'm just saying when you're ready, I'm here if you want. In the meantime, let's get this woman back in her own house where she can boss the two of us around properly." He winked and grabbed the suitcase from the bed.

Murphy looked at Ivy and rolled her eyes. "Yep. I get it, Aunt Ivy. He really should use those powers for good!" The women shared a laugh making Phantom grin.

CHAPTER FORTY-FIVE

STRIKER MADE an offer on the property and within three days, it had been accepted and he held the keys and the deed. He was alone at the property for the time being. Phantom was taking care of Ivy this morning and promised Striker he'd be there around noon. Striker had spent most of the morning at the local big box store stocking up on cleaning supplies, paint, brushes, rollers, and everything else they would need. He unpacked his truck and threw his jacket over the bar. He was going to start there. He had contacted the water, electric and gas companies the day before, making arrangements to have everything switched to his name. He walked over to the thermostat and checked to make sure it was on and then checked the water. Having made sure they were good, he ran a bucket of hot, soapy water and set it on the floor beside the bar. He walked to the jukebox, blew the dust away and put in a coin. *Let's just see.* Sure, enough, the jukebox whirred to life and Brooks and Dunn started singing about a red dirt road. Satisfied with that, Striker got down to the business of scrubbing the bar.

He didn't know how long he'd been working but it surprised him a little when the front door opened and

Phantom strolled in. Phantom, paused, then grinned as he heard the jukebox playing some kickass country tune. He danced over to the bar where Striker stood rolling his eyes. "Save it for the ladies, asshole." Striker followed that up with his own trademark grin.

Phantom took in the bar where all the years of dirt and grease had built up. "Wow, man! Nice job! This thing looks even better than I thought it would!"

"Oh, ye of little faith. We're gonna have the best pub around!" He let Phantom know he had taken care of the gas, water and electricity and Phantom nodded his approval. "I gotta admit, I was surprised as hell when the jukebox worked!"

"Everything's falling into place, that's for sure." Phantom saw a shadow briefly pass over his friend's face. *Well, maybe not everything.* "Listen, man. Don't go all crazy on me, but Ivy said Murphy thinks you've left town. What the fuck? Don't you think maybe you should do something like, I don't know, tell her you're here?"

"You know as well as I do that I can't just ring her up. She's good and pissed and blaming me for everything. But, I have a plan and it's gonna include you and the rest of our friends. But first, let's get this place up and running."

Phantom grabbed another bucket, filled it with water and floor cleaner, and with a mop in one hand and the bucket in the other, headed to the stage and dance floor area. Between the two of them, they had the bar area and the stage/dance floor area done by the end of the afternoon. Pleased with their progress, they decided to call it a day. At least Phantom did. He wanted to get home so he could prepare a dinner for Ivy. Striker planned to come back after having a bite to eat and do a bit more. Yep, he planned to get this place up and running and then he was getting his woman back.

CHAPTER FORTY-SIX

WHEN PHANTOM GOT to the cottage, Murphy was there banging around in the kitchen. Ivy was settled on the couch with a blanket and a pillow from the bed, scowling towards the kitchen entrance. Phantom knelt beside Ivy. "I'd like to kiss you, Darlin, but with that look on your face, I'm not sure I'd come back in one piece."

She smiled then. "Sorry. I just don't like not being able to do what I want in my own damn kitchen!"

He leaned in and kissed her soundly. "Just relax. Murphy and I have this. Speaking of which, let me go in and see what she needs." Ivy watched as he swaggered into the kitchen, feeling much better now that he was here.

He rounded the corner of the kitchen doorway and almost collided with Murphy, who was headed in to Ivy with a cup of tea in her hands. The teacup shook and he grabbed her arms to steady her. "Sorry, Murph. Didn't know you were comin' this way."

"No damage done." She said as she noticed none of the tea had splashed out. "I wasn't sure what time you would be here so I started some Chicken Marsala with a side of noodles. Just let them cook until the timer goes off. Now, I'll get out of your hair.

"Just a wait a minute!" His voice had an edge to it he hadn't really expected. Murphy hadn't either from the surprised look on her face. "Sorry. Didn't mean to sound so gruff, but I want you to stay. I'd like to tell you about what I've been working on. Stay and haver dinner with us?" He raised his eyebrows, waiting for an answer.

"I just figured you'd like to be alone with Ivy. But, I can stay if you want." She almost sounded relieved.

"You know, just because you're mad at a friend of mine, doesn't mean *we're* not friends," he said, making a back and forth motion between the two of them. She smiled. "Well, then, *friend*, move your ass out of the way so I can get this tea to Ivy before it gets cold!" Phantom made a show of stepping aside and bowing as she walked by.

He set the table in the kitchen and brought the food over after the timer went off. Ivy and Murphy were already seated and he joined them. It was time to let Murphy know about what he was doing, but not who he was doing it with. "So," he said as he got Murphy's attention. "Ivy's already aware, but I wanted to let you know I'm going to be opening a neighborhood pub." He proceeded to tell her about his (and Striker's) plans and how it was going so far. He assured her that either one of them could reach him on his cell when he was working, but if she wanted to move in with them temporarily, he would be good with that, too. Murphy was very supportive, even going so far as to offer to help him clean and paint, but he assured her he wanted to do this and he would appreciate the help with Ivy more. She decided to move in for however long it would take so he could concentrate on getting the business up and running. After dinner, he shooed her out to pack her bags while he cleaned up the kitchen.

CHAPTER FORTY-SEVEN

THE NEXT DAY was Sunday so Phantom kissed Ivy goodbye early knowing Murphy would take care of her needs, and headed towards the pub. Even though it was early, Striker was already there scrubbing the kitchen stove top. Phantom strode in and placed a to-go cup in front of his friend. He had stopped on his way in and got them both coffees. "Morning." Phantom said. "Looks like this place is really coming along. You must have worked late last night to finish the bar room."

Striker raised his cup in a thank you salute. "Yeah. Remember, I don't have anything else I have to do and, the sooner we get this place ready, the sooner I can get my woman back."

"About that," Phantom rubbed his hand over his stubbled chin, "during dinner last night, I let Murphy know that I was working on opening a neighborhood pub. I basically told her everything about what we are doing except I left out the 'we' part. She's under the impression it's just me." He chuckled a little about the next part. "She actually offered to help me clean and paint. I thought about saying yes knowing she'd run in to you but...you have a plan and we'll stick to that. Speaking of which, just what is this brilliant plan of yours anyway?'

Striker leaned back on their newly cleaned stove and took a sip of his coffee. "Here's how I see it. We get the place ready to open but before opening day, we – as in you – throw a celebration party for our – as in your – friends, including Murphy. She comes in and sees that I'm here and planning to stick around. The plan might need a little work, but..."

Phantom leaned against the doorjamb eyeing his friend. "It just might work. How long do you think it's gonna take to get this place ready?"

"I've been doing some calculating in my head. Since I don't have any other responsibilities at this time, I'm planning on doing the bulk of the work. I've ordered chairs, booths, pool tables. I think we should replace the bar stools. We'll need glasses and things for the bar. I've been in touch with vendors. Well, here..." he pulled a notebook out from under his coat in the corner. "I've been making lists. You and I will do the cleaning and painting together plus Riley and Cassie offered to help out and I took them up on it. In fact, they should be here any minute. So, to answer your question, I was hoping we could push it and have the party for New Year's Eve. I think with our friend's help, we should be able to accomplish all the cleaning today and start on the painting."

Phantom looked impressed. "You sure have done your homework, my friend. Did you decide on colors, or do you want my help with that?"

"Don't forget I've been thinking about this pub for much longer than you. I started some of those lists months ago. As for colors, I already picked up some paint and it's out behind the bar. I don't think you'll have any problems with it. Going with neutrals appealing to both sexes. Now you can tell me how fucking brilliant I really am." They were both laughing when Riley and Cassie walked in.

The four of them went to work on the cleaning first. Within two hours, the place shined like a new penny. Striker went around opening paint cans and marking them for each wall and they had the kitchen and bar area painted in no time. Striker and Phantom stood in the bar area and couldn't help grinning. It was really coming together and so much faster than either of them had thought. He had contacted a contractor to do the outside and he was going to be starting the next day. Luckily, the weather had cooperated. He had chosen to have the outside done in deep blue shingle design with an ivory trim and deep purple door. Now, he wanted to talk to Cassie about bringing to life his idea of a sign. She, being artist extraordinaire, would be the one he thought would get his vision. "After I talk to Cassie about the sign, I'm gonna head out for some grub. Why don't you pack it in tonight, brother, and go home to see about that woman of yours?"

"Sounds good." She's doing well but I have to be careful not to coddle her too much or she's just like a cat in a tree!" He chuckled. "The place is looking good. It feels good to have a different purpose. Thanks, man." He clapped Striker on the back, said his goodbyes to Riley and Cassie who were finishing up in the kitchen, and went to look after Ivy.

Striker strode into the kitchen where his friends were cleaning brushes and rollers. He spoke to Cassie about the signage he had in mind and she was completely on board. They finished their clean up and, before leaving, told Striker that with Christmas just a few weeks away, they expected him for Christmas dinner. He thanked them and they left with Cassie promising to get working on the signage right away. Striker walked around his place and felt a sense of accomplishment, a sense of pride. He may be able to pull this off by New Year's Eve after all.

CHAPTER FORTY-EIGHT

CHRISTMAS EVE came around and Murphy was feeling lower than she ever had. Justice was never far from her mind even though she knew she would never see him again. Even with his best friends here, there was no reason to see her. Even if he came back to visit them, he wouldn't seek her out. And the way she demanded they not talk about him in front of her? They certainly wouldn't mention if he was in town. Had she misjudged him? Every day she asked herself this same question. Every day she wondered if she had made a mistake. Every day she missed him just a little bit more.

Phantom had carried in a large tree a week or so ago and Murphy had decorated it with a little help from Ivy. Ivy was getting along well but she still tired easily. They placed the tree in the living room where her desk normally sat in the bay window. Colored lights adorned it along with old and new ornaments including some Murphy had made when she was a little girl. Murphy had placed garland on the mantel and there was a fire burning in the fireplace. Their usual tradition was to order pizza in on Christmas Eve since Christmas Day would be about the cooking. Phantom liked the idea so pizzas were ordered and drinks were served. Ivy had gotten off all the pain medication she had been on in the hospital so she happily accepted the glass of wine Phantom poured for her. Christmas music was playing from the radio in the kitchen, making Murphy even more melancholy. She looked up and searched the face of Justice's best friend. He had been true to his word and never mentioned him. But she needed to know. "Phantom," her voice was husky and tears were shining in her eyes. "I know I asked you not to mention Justice to me and I appreciate that you haven't. But I need to know. I feel I might have misjudged the situation and, even though he probably will never want to see me again, I..." a sob broke from her and her chin bent to her chest, shoulders shaking.

Phantom exchanged a knowing look with Ivy. He rose from his chair and sat next to Murphy on the couch, putting a strong arm around her. He had come to think of her as his niece, too. "I don't think Striker would feel like you say he would. He cares about you too much." With this her head shot up to look into his eyes. "You know where he is?" The hopeful look on her face made Phantom and Ivy exchange that look again. He took a deep breath before speaking. "I know where he is, Murph, but just like he gave you time, you need to give him some space, too. Remember when I told you things will work out? Trust in that, Darlin'. The holidays are filled with miracles." He winked at Ivy, squeezed Murphy's shoulder and got up to answer the door when the pizza guy knocked.

CHAPTER FORTY-NINE

CHRISTMAS DAY at the cottage was filled with music, food and laughter. Murphy was feeling a little better having gotten some of her worries off her chest the night before. Ivy was able to help a bit more today without tiring too much. Murphy stopped to watch her and Phantom in the kitchen together. They were laughing and cooking and every now and then a song would strike him and he would lead her into a dance, sometimes fast, sometimes slow and sometimes he carefully dipped her while she swatted him with her 'good' arm. Murphy wanted this. She wanted this with Justice.

Christmas came to Riley's penthouse, too. He and Cassie had decorated a huge tree and there were twinkling white lights everywhere! Striker had shown up as requested. In fact, they had threatened him that they would come and get his ass if it wasn't at their house by one o'clock in the afternoon! Cassie wasn't the best of cooks but Riley was! There was a Christmas ham with all the fixings. The drinks flowed freely and Striker allowed himself to relax and take the entire day off. It would have been the perfect day if only he had Murphy. Soon. Very soon. After dinner was eaten and the kitchen cleaned up, Cassie dragged Striker into what he thought was an extra bedroom. His eyes grew wide when they walked in. Cassie had set this up as her art studio and, as promised, she had been working furiously on the sign for the pub. It was exquisite! Even more perfect than he had imagined it. And she had even arranged to have it installed the next day.

CHAPTER FIFTY

THE DAY AFTER Christmas had Striker up and out early. He arrived at the pub before dawn. After unlocking the door, he allowed himself the pleasure of looking around at all their hard work. He had pushed himself and called in some favors and it was almost finished.

Anyone seeing the place before would not recognize it now. New tables were arranged in the bar area along with matching stools pulled up against the bar. The walls were the color of sand and glasses and decanters glistened from the shelves on the wall behind the bar. The mahogany bar was a showpiece, updated with a new copper foot railing wrapped around its bottom. On the other side of the room, the dance floor and stage area glittered with tiny lights and polished wood. He was home. It was all coming together. Phantom had invited everyone for New Year's Eve, telling them he wanted to christen the place with his friends and family before opening it to the public. Of course, everyone knew Striker would be there, too. Everyone that is, but Murphy.

Striker sauntered into the kitchen, flipping the lights on as he went. The stove tops and oven had still been in good condition. They just had needed cleaned and checked. The walls in the kitchen had been painted a coral color with copper cookware and plates the sand color matching the bar room walls. The lights danced across the kitchen surfaces, making the copper look extra rich.

He moved on to the back room where he had placed three pool tables and another jukebox found on Ebay. Benches had been installed along the walls. This was one of his favorite rooms. The walls were a warm tan color and the ceiling was copper. A large stone fireplace ran along one wall and Striker had placed two leather club chairs in front, one on each side. This was a man's room but he would make damn sure women felt welcome, and safe, too.

Each bathroom had been redone, using marble and the best fixtures he could find. Hell, these bathrooms were nicer than most bathrooms he'd seen in houses! He was truly happy with the outcome. His dream was coming true. As he walked through to the bar area, his phone pinged. He removed it from his back pocket and checked the text. It was Cassie, asking if he was ready for the install of the sign. He texted back he would be there in twenty minutes.

As he walked outside, he was surprised to see that it had gotten light out. The sun wasn't up quite yet but it was light enough to see. The outside of the building looked great in that deep blue. The shingles had been put on just right. All that was left was the sign, and he hoped it would blow everybody away!

Cassie had not only done the sign, but she had arranged the installation with someone she had worked with before. She knew he was not only good, but reliable. He had shown up at Riley's penthouse right on time and she was showing him the design when Striker sauntered in. She had needed Striker as muscle to get the sign in the vehicle that would carry it to the pub.

Once at the pub site, they showed the installer where and how they wanted it and he got to work. An hour later, done! Striker and Cassie stood in the parking lot and checked out the building. It was everything he had hoped for and more.

CHAPTER FIFTY-ONE

THE WEEK BETWEEN Christmas and New Year's Eve passed in a blur. Striker and Phantom were busy getting last minute party plans finished. Ivy was hitting therapy hard with her usual zest for life. Cassie and Riley were doing whatever they could to help everyone out. Everyone was happy and in holiday mode. Everyone, that is, except Murphy. She was trying. She really was. She put on a smile but it felt like she was just going through the motions. She had sent away the only man she ever loved. Yes. *Loved.* And this was the holidays. Her favorite time of the year. No matter what had happened before in her life, the holidays always fixed it for her. Not this time. They couldn't fix this.

It was New Year's Eve and Murphy knew life had to go on. She was determined to put on a pretty party dress and smile and support someone who had become very special to her. Phantom. Not only did her aunt love him, but she did, too. He had become her honorary uncle and he had a special place in her heart. He was a complete alpha male, protective, loving, funny, tender. Shit! Now she was thinking of Justice. Again. She pushed the memory aside and dressed for the party. The dress she chose was red with a fitted bodice and full skirt hitting her at mid-thigh. She paired it with a pair of black ankle boots sporting a killer set of stiletto heels. She allowed her hair to fall in natural waves to her shoulders and applied make-up to her eyes so they would have a smoky look. She looked fantastic. Now, if she could keep a smile on her face, she just might fool everyone into thinking she felt that way, too.

Cassie and Riley were picking Murphy and Ivy up at seven pm sharp. Cassie looked great, as usual, in her black mini-dress. It was covered with sequins that only Cassie could pull off. Her over-the-knee boots were red with what had to be four-inch heels and she had matched them with red earrings and bangles jingling on her wrist. Ivy appeared at the bottom of the stairs in a gold wrap-dress, making her look even curvier than she already was. The knee length dress dipped in the front showing just the right amount of cleavage and her shoes with their two-inch heels, were strappy and matched the gold in the dress perfectly! Phantom's tongue was going to be hanging out all night! And let's not forget Riley. Riley was handsome no matter what he wore, but tonight he was exceptional! He had on a tux with a black shirt and red tie. Together, he and Cassie looked like something straight out of GQ!

Riley had gotten a limo for them tonight and they all piled into the car and rode to the pub. Murphy's intake of breath could be heard as they pulled into the parking lot. It was exquisite! The sky was twinkling with stars and the building was lit perfectly. The limo driver opened the car door for them and Murphy and Ivy linked arms and just stood staring at the building. The deep blue shingles had a faint sheen to them from the landscape lighting. The purple door held a large holiday wreath. Directly above the door was a faint neon sign done in the same purple as the door that will say 'pub is open'. But then, the best part was the sign at the top of the building. It was done in cursive, a beautiful script with no capitals, just one word...imps. Imps? She'd definitely have to ask Phantom about that! The sign was lit up with colors like she had never seen before. It started out with a beautiful dark blue then it morphed into a purple and then ended in red. It all looked like a little jewel box! As she was staring, speechless, Phantom came out through the door, looking outstandingly handsome in his own tux, and welcomed everyone. The moment his eyes fell on Ivy, Yep! Tongue hanging out! His eyes moved over her body like physical touch. Riley cleared his throat. "Uh, want us to give you some privacy there, old man?" That was enough to shake Phantom out of it but he never took his eyes off Ivy. He just replied "Yeah. Would you?" The men chuckled and the women rolled their eyes, even though the smiles never left their faces.

Phantom positioned himself between Murphy and Ivy, keeping an arm around Ivy's waist, he addressed Murphy. "So, what do you think of the place?"

"I never dreamed you were doing something so...so...beautiful! I'm overwhelmed! There's just one thing I have to ask. Uh...imps?"

Phantom gave a low husky laugh. I'll explain but let's first get inside. Looks like it's starting to snow." Murphy thought the building had a magical quality with the first snowflakes swirling around it.

They stepped inside the warmth of the building and once again, the beauty was overwhelming. The place shimmered with white mini-lights, the wood glowed, the mirrors sparkled. Murphy was taking it all in when her eye caught movement by the bar. Silver eyes! Silver eyes staring directly at her! She couldn't move. Hell, she couldn't *breathe!* The background just faded away. The people around her faded away. There was only Justice. Only Justice with his handsome face and silver eyes in a black on black tux, shirt and tie. He pushed off the bar and swaggered towards her. She felt as though she couldn't stand a second longer when he was directly in front of her. Inches in front of her. Staring at her, *through* her with those damn silver eyes!

"Murphy." It was almost a whisper. It took a moment for her to realize he had used her first name. She was having a hard time seeing him through the tears gathering in her eyes. She tried to blink them away but one fell and was rolling down her cheek. Justice's warm hand was suddenly on her face, wiping at the tear. "Murphy." He said again, almost like a prayer, a plea. Then, she smiled. Boy, did she smile! "Justice. I can't believe you're here!"

Justice's other hand came up to frame her face. "I never left. I wasn't ever planning to leave. This is my place. Phantom is my partner." Murphy was trying to take it all in. He was here! He was staying! "I knew you needed time so I threw myself into making this what I wanted. I asked everyone to keep it secret until I could show it to you myself."

It was then that Murphy remembered there were other people in the room. Her gaze met each one individually. The smiles on their faces matched hers and, yes, the tears in the eyes of the women matched hers, too. "You all knew?" Each of them nodded and Ivy pulled tissues from her purse, handing them out to the other ladies. Murphy's gaze landed on Phantom. "So... imps?"

Phantom chuckled as only he could and looked at Striker. "You'll have to ask the boss. I didn't know about it myself until today."

Striker's grin had come out in full force, knowing Murphy had forgiven him. "Imps" he said, his eyes never leaving Murphy's. "Ivy, Murphy, Phantom, Striker... the initials spell imps." With that, his lips clamped down on Murphy's while everyone laughed and hooted around them. When they broke their kiss, they declared their love for each other silently, and with a huge smile and still tears in her eyes, she looked at the people surrounding her, and recognized family, love and home.

Thank you for choosing **Justice Prevails**. If you enjoyed it, please leave a review on Amazon. A review does more than what most people realize.

Continue with the IMPS romance trilogy by choosing the second book in the story, **Phantom Rising,** featuring Phantom and Ivy.

I love hearing from my readers. If you'd like to contact me, I can be reached by email at sommersbambi@gmail.com.

Thanks again! Happy reading!!

Bambi

The IMPS Trilogy includes:
    Justice Prevails (book one)
    Phantom Rising (book two)
    Remembering Riley (book three)

Also, by Bambi Sommers:
    Firebird
    Firebird 2
All books available as ebook or paperback on Amazon.com.

Join my newsletter on my website at bambisommers.com and you'll be the first to know of new books!

Also, visit Bambi's author page on Amazon and Bookbub or find her on Facebook, Twitter, and Instagram.

Made in the USA
Middletown, DE
06 October 2018